LUCY'S HEARTH

A MORGAN'S FIRE ROMANCE

M. LEE PRESCOTT

Lucy's Hearth

A Morgan's Fire Romance

By
M. Lee Prescott

Published by Mt. Hope Press
Copyright 2019, M. Lee Prescott
Cover Design by Ashley Lopez
Formatting by E-book Formatting Fairies
ISBN: 978-0-9982184-7-2

AUTHOR WEBSITE

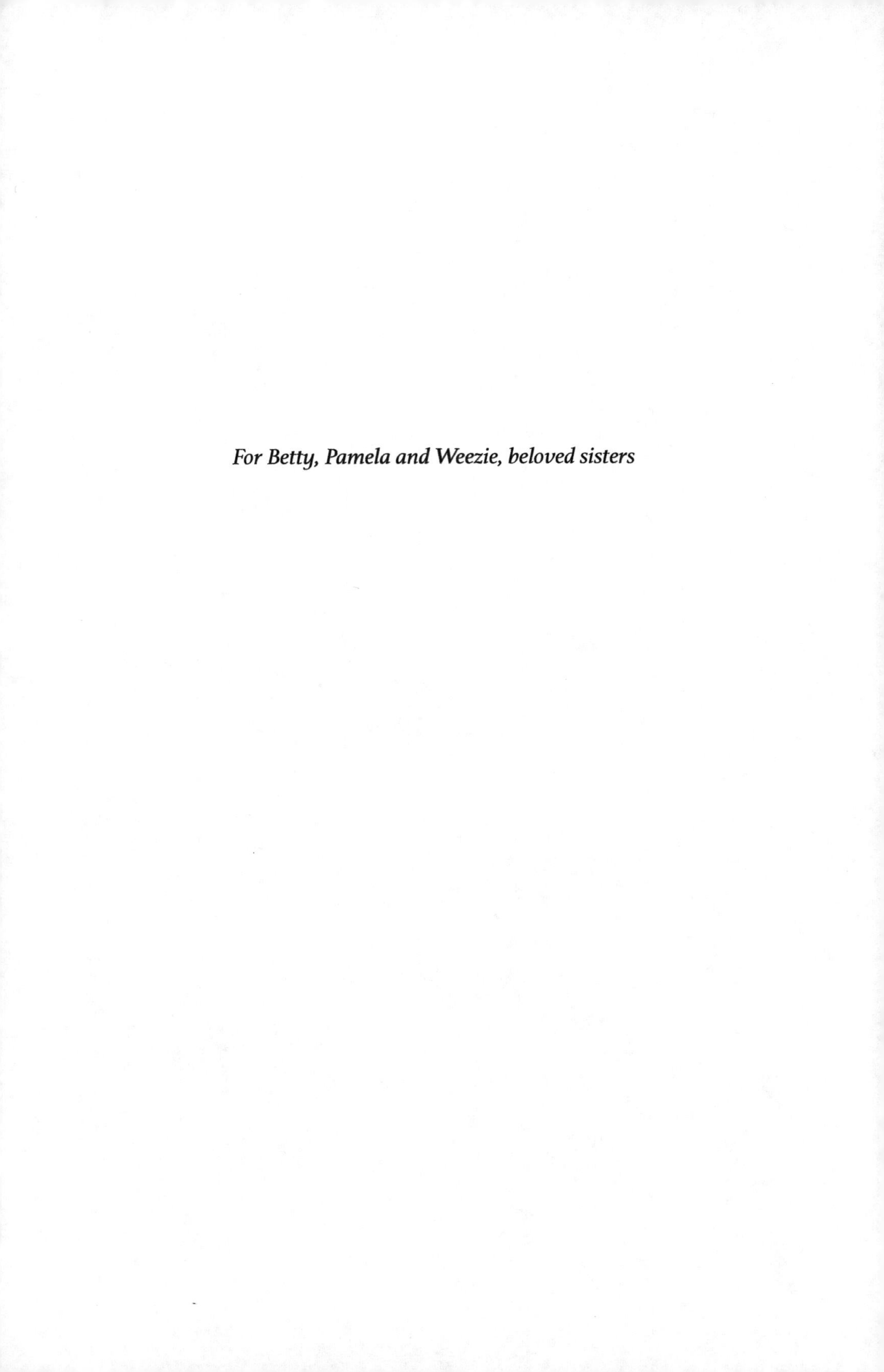

For Betty, Pamela and Weezie, beloved sisters

CHAPTER 1

Lucy came home to an empty house. She had really enjoyed having Gus Casey staying in the apartment over the garage. Now he was gone, back to his job at Valley Stables in Arizona. She thought back to the week in Saguaro Valley with her mother, where she'd met Richard Morgan, the man with whom she had just gone riding.

How do I feel about Richard? The longing in his coal-black eyes as he helped her off her horse. She knew he wanted to kiss her, but she had pulled back. *Why? I'm attracted to him, so why not? He's good-looking, filthy rich, and fun. But love? That was with Rob. Our love was supposed to last forever. Instead, my heart's in a million pieces, and I'm not sure how to pick them up.* Her sister Harriet's recommendation was to see Elise, her therapist. *What could be easier?*

She and Rob had met in college when he was a struggling pre-med student. They married during his residency. Rob's parents, now deceased, had built the home Lucy shared with her two teenagers. It was left to Rob and his older sister, Corky, along with another house on Cape Cod. Upon the parents' death, Corky had insisted on having the Cape Cod house, which she promptly sold for an enormous sum. Then, proceeds in hand, she moved to California to become an actress. Last they heard she was out of money and no closer to an acting career than when she had left New England.

Rob and Lucy lovingly restored every inch of the rambling Dutch colonial. Its exquisite woodwork and fine details gave it the appearance of an antique home. Most of the furniture—excepting the most valuable pieces, which Corky had also insisted upon having —had stayed with the house. There were five bedrooms on the second floor. The master suite at one end and then Robert's and Amy's rooms at the other. They kept one room as a guest room and the fifth bedroom had been converted into an office for Lucy's business, a mail-order catalog, Merlin's Closet, specializing in children's books. Now booming, her business had since moved to office space in town.

Lucy looked for a note but found nothing on the kitchen counter except an assortment of dirty dishes, empty milk cartons, and scattered crumbs. She liked a well-ordered house where everything had its place and where one could relax in serenity, not chaos. The first floor of the house had a huge kitchen-family room, a stone hearth at one end, and a recently completed bay window addition at the other. They ate most meals in the light-filled breakfast nook, seated around a burnished maple oval table. On either side of the bay window were two narrow leaded glass panels made by her mother, deep blue morning glories twined round each other reaching toward the sun.

A large family room, smaller wood-paneled den, and solarium were at one end of the house. Off the kitchen was a formal dining room with a fieldstone fireplace, and behind the kitchen, a laundry room, mud room, and bath, as well as a cubbyhole of a room that Rob had used as his home office. A comfortable house, Lucy prided herself on making it even more so in the fifteen years she had lived there.

As she straightened the den, the back door slammed. She paused. "Hi, I'm back here. That you, Rob?" she called, listening for her son's voice.

"It's me, Mom!" her daughter Amy called, popping her head

around the den door as her mother scooped up a pile of Sunday papers.

"Hi sweetie, where've you been?" Papers put aside, she hugged her fourteen-year-old.

"At the Robinsons'. They're going out to dinner, so I came home. They asked me to go, but I thought I'd better not 'cause I couldn't get you on the phone. How was your ride?"

"Bumpy."

"You've been spending a lot of time with Mr. Morgan, huh?"

"Some. Is that okay with you?"

"Course, what do you think?"

"It's just...with your dad and all."

"Dad has hideous Chloe, so why shouldn't you date?"

"Now, now." Lucy loaded Amy up with an armful of papers and watched her head into the kitchen. Her hair, so like her grandmother's and her Aunt Harriet's, trailed in one thick chestnut braid to her waist. She even walked like Helen, as Lucy herself did. While Lucy favored her father in appearance, with the same pale blue eyes and sandy hair, her gait and mannerisms were her mother's and now, her daughter's as well. Amy most definitely had the Gifford swagger. It suited her.

"Aunt Harriet called," Amy said over her shoulder. "She's stopping by."

"Thanks, sweetie!"

RICHARD MORGAN DROVE UP TO HIS SPRAWLING FARMHOUSE, THE FIRST building completed on the property just north of Horseshoe Crab Cove. Fifty-three years old, he had been a widower for nearly two decades. Since his wife's death, he hadn't met anyone like Lucy Winthrop Brennan. She was the first woman since Laura with whom he could imagine sharing his life. He'd dated, so many he'd lost count, but those relationships petered out after a few months.

There is something about Lucy. A wounded bird, yes, but with a depth of soul. He sat on the porch glider and closed his eyes, picturing her soft peach skin, sky-blue eyes, and the way she crinkled her nose when she smiled. He longed to stroke her slender arms, or better yet, drape them over his shoulders and draw her close, but he sensed she wouldn't welcome such gestures. As he let out a deep sigh, a voice called.

"Hey, Dad! You awake?" Weezie, his youngest daughter, bounded up on the porch, followed by her brother Rich, his eldest. Rich was CEO of Morgan Enterprises. He oversaw all his father's businesses, including the new farm. Behind the others came Gail, one of his middle children. Gail and Weezie still lived at home. Gail did publicity and odd jobs for Morgan Enterprises. Richard was constantly encouraging her to spread her wings, but so far, she hadn't wanted to leave the nest.

Richard grinned. "Well, well, well, to what do I owe this pleasure? Are you triple teaming me this morning?"

"Something like that," Rich said, pushing a lock of long sandy hair from his forehead as he set down a bulging briefcase. "Don't you remember? We're having a business meeting." Rich was Laura's child. Same smile, same sandy hair, Laura's soft hazel eyes. He also had her quiet, steady temperament, which made him so effective in his job as CEO.

"Dad's head is in the clouds, daydreaming about his new girlfriend," Weezie said in a singsong voice.

Gail rolled her eyes. "Don't be ridiculous."

Weezie stuck out her tongue at her sister.

Richard threw his hands up. "Okay, okay, girls. No squabbling. Come on inside."

He put his arm around Gail, whom he called his little hedgehog. She'd always been his prickly child. Ninety percent of the time, Gail's brow was wrinkled with a frown. He wished he could change that, but for twenty-six years, he'd been largely unsuccessful. Weezie pushed by, swinging open the door with a flourish, receiving another eye roll from her sister. A study in contrasts, the sisters. Weezie, petite and slender, her dark brown hair cut short in a stylish pixie bob, chocolate eyes dancing with light. Gail, short too, but all curves, with hazel eyes, her shoulder-length auburn hair held back by a slim leather headband, and freckles splayed across her nose. They both had cute turned-up noses, but the resemblance ended there. Audrey Hepburn and Rita Hayworth, Richard sometimes called them.

Once the four were seated at the dining room table with coffee or water, Richard said, "You're the boss, Rich. Why don't you get us started."

Rich pulled several folders from his briefcase. "Thanks, Dad. So... construction is pretty much on schedule for this first phase. Barns are looking great. Gus ordered most of the equipment and tack before he left."

"Gee, I wish we could've persuaded him to stay longer," Richard said. "But my brother and his partner would have sued the pants off me, I'm afraid. He was perfect for the job."

"Which we're having trouble filling," Rich said.

Weezie looked at Richard. "I can run the mustang program."

"You're a terrific rider, baby," he said. "But the job takes skills you don't have. Not yet, at least."

His youngest huffed. "Do too."

"Besides, you've got school."

"I'm taking a leave." Weezie was enrolled in a master's program for social work, but so far, her participation had been minimal.

"Can we please move on?" Gail said.

"Not until I've said my piece," Weezie said.

Rich sat calmly, shuffling through a file. "Dad, I'll defer to you on this. Are we going to discuss who's running the mustang rescue now?"

"No, except to hear if you've got any good candidates." Weezie opened her mouth, and he raised a hand. "Have you?"

"Couple of guys are interviewing tomorrow. Gail and I can handle it. Weezie's welcome to come, and I may ask Dennis to step in since he's the one who worked most closely with Gus."

"Not true," Weezie said. "I spent every day with Gus and the horses."

Smiling at his youngest, Richard said, "Let's talk about where we are with the thoroughbreds."

"Scouts are looking. It's not easy. Uncle Ben and his buddy grabbed up some of the best this past year for Valley Stables."

"Gail, where are we with branding? We've gotta come up with a name for this enterprise before long, or no one's gonna pay us a bit of attention."

"We're working on it, Dad, I promise. Morgan's Run East isn't gonna cut it, though."

"Agreed," her father said. "What about the wild horses? Where are we with them?"

"Gus thought we should start with no more than five mustangs, but there's such a pressing need for rescue."

"Think we could push that to ten?" Richard asked.

"Not without a competent experienced trainer," Rich said.

"Maybe I can get Gus to come back for a month or so this winter."

Weezie shook her head. "Not a chance, Dad. He's moved into his beautiful new house, kids are happy, and he's getting married soon."

They talked awhile longer, then Weezie and Rich departed. Gail stayed behind to discuss publicity. Finally, she stood. "I'm going into the Cove. You need anything?"

"Thanks, sweetie, I'm fine. I may persuade Lucy to have dinner with me later, but Callie can fix you girls something."

Gail frowned at the mention of Lucy Brennan. "Mom would have loved it here."

He patted her hand. "Maybe. She sure loved Maine after all our years as vagabonds." As he watched Gail gather her things, he thought, *If I get serious with Lucy, my little hedgehog is going to pull out all the stops to break it up.*

CHAPTER 2

Lucy's partner, Lolly LaSalle, was surrounded by a wall of boxes when Lucy arrived at the office, lunches from the Cove Grille in hand. "I see you've been consorting with the enemy," Lolly said, noticing the bags. Her ex-in-laws, Rosa and Cesar Rodriguez, owned the Grille. Lolly remained friendly with the couple and several of their offspring, but rarely patronized their very popular restaurant for fear of running into her ex. Sandy Rodriguez, her former husband, lived in town and ran a music venue, Sandy's, on the coast north of the village.

"Only way you'll get your favorite sandwich," Lucy said, plunking a bag in front of her.

Lolly rubbed her hands together. "Thank you, thank you! I have dreams about the California burger."

Lucy grabbed two iced teas out of the office fridge and came to join her. "You might need to get a life, then."

"Says you."

"Touché." Lucy smiled, gazing around at their surroundings. "We really need an assistant. We can afford it. We could go after someone who loves books or just hire some muscle for all this. A few hours a week would really help with this mess."

"If it's muscle you want, we could put a notice up in Averill's," Lolly said, referring to the village's general store.

"Or I could ask Rob if any of his friends would be interested. He's been working after school for his father, so I can't ask him to do this too."

"We could beg him to quit that job and come here."

"No, thanks. Last thing I want is for him to be in the middle of a turf war."

Lucy's ex-husband, Rob, was an internist and ran a family medical practice in the village. He had two associates, and between them, several nurse practitioners and three nurses, they served a number of towns north and south of the village. They maintained their office here because it was central and cheaper. Lucy spent part of every day wishing Rob would move somewhere else, preferably Timbuktu.

"What's new with the unmentionable anyway?" Lolly asked.

"Nothing I want to know about."

"What about the creepy girlfriend."

Lucy put up her hand. "Stop! New subject."

Lolly gave her a mischievous look. "Okay, so what's up with Mr. Hunky Farmer?"

"Nothing. We're friends."

"Does he know that?"

"No, but I'm going tell him tonight. I'm just not ready for more."

"Is it because your ex is still lurking around?"

"No." Lucy threw her sandwich wrapper into the trash. "Let's talk about the mess that's surrounding us, okay?"

"You mean your idiot doctor and my sleazy music promoter?"

"Enough! I'm going to start unpacking these. We've got orders up the wazoo, and some of them need to go out today."

Hands on hips, Lolly stood beside her. "Fine, fine, grouchy, but I want to hear all about your hot date tonight."

"I'm not listening!"

∼

"You look nice, Mom," Amy said as Lucy came downstairs to wait for Richard. "Is Mr. Morgan picking you up?"

"Yes, in about ten minutes. You gonna be okay till Rob gets home?"

Her daughter rolled her eyes. "Mom!"

"Sorry. I'm surprised you didn't join your brother and Dad for dinner. They went to the Clam Shack, I think."

"I have a ton of homework."

"But you have to eat."

"And I did. The leftover lasagna and salad was perfect."

"Okay, I was just wondering, 'cause you love the Clam Shack."

"Yeah, but I hate Chloe, and I didn't want to sit through another dinner listening to what a great massage therapist she is. Yuck!"

Lucy smiled, ruffling her daughter's hair. "You don't have to hate Chloe for my sake."

"Don't worry. She's detestable enough on her own, believe me. She's a complete bitch. I don't know what Dad sees in her."

Youth, Lucy mused. *Youth, energy, new and exciting.* "Well, sweetie, I see Richard's car. I'll be back early."

"Don't hurry home on my account!" Amy called as she closed the front door.

"Wow, you look spectacular!" Richard said as she strolled down the front walk.

Lucy smiled. She'd taken great care with her casual outfit, choosing a top and slacks that flattered her slim figure and silver and lapis jewelry that brought out the blue in her eyes.

"Thanks, so do you."

And he did in slacks and a dark-green linen sports shirt. Like his brother Ben, Richard looked fifteen years younger than he was, with craggy chiseled features, a strong jawline, and those eyebrows, dark like his eyes. He kissed her lightly on the cheek, then escorted her to the car, one hand on the small of her back. His touch was light but firm. After a year of raw nerves, sadness, and grief, his touch was comforting. Lucy felt safe for the first time in many months.

∾

RICHARD PEERED AROUND THE COVE GRILLE. THE DÉCOR WAS A MIX OF nautical and Hispanic, but somehow it worked. They were seated by the window overlooking the harbor. "So this is my first time here. What's good?"

"Everything. Cesar and Rosa are amazing cooks. I always get seafood, but people love the pasta dishes and the enchiladas and all. You really can't go wrong."

"It's a pretty eclectic menu, isn't it?"

"Changes every month."

"Hi, guys, I'm Carla." A pretty twenty-something dressed in denim capris and a gingham top greeted them, pad in hand. Pencil stuck in her ponytail, she pulled it out, unleashing a strand of auburn curls. "Can I start you with a drink?"

"You're new," Lucy said, smiling at her.

"Yup, just started this week. Love it." She bent down and whispered, "My boyfriend Sandy's parents own it."

Richard suggested they get a bottle of wine, and after Lucy's approval, Carla disappeared.

"Oh gee," she said. *Poor Lolly!*

"Second thoughts about the wine?" he asked, concern in his gaze.

"No, the wine's perfect. Our perky waitress is apparently dating my partner's ex. Kind of an ongoing nightmare."

He smiled. "Perky's a perfect description. I would imagine it's rough in a small town after a divorce."

She nodded. "Yes."

"Still difficult for you? I hear that your former husband is the town doc."

"One of them. I have my moments," she answered truthfully. "But it is what it is. If you'd asked me a year ago, I'd have given you a different answer, and if you ask me three years from now, there'll probably be yet another. It's a process, grieving for what's lost forever. People say it takes five years to feel normal again, so I've got a ways to go."

He reached across the table and took her hand. "I'm sorry."

"Thanks. I'm working on it. That's the best I can say. Now let's talk about something more interesting. Tell me about the farm and how things are going. You had just gotten started on our ride."

Carla returned and poured the wine, after which they each ordered the seafood special, pistachio-crusted sea bass, then chatted amiably about their days, his hopes for the farm, and Lucy's business. "We really need to hire an assistant," she said, setting down her fork. "This fish is delicious, isn't it?"

"Yes, it is, and I might know someone."

"Oh?"

"My son Wolfie. Did you meet him at the wedding?"

"Just for a minute," she said, "then I never saw him again."

Richard smiled. "That's Wolfie. He's an introvert. Hermit might be more like it. Weezie's the opposite. I was surprised when he said he wanted to come with us to the wedding, but I think it was an opportunity to see that part of the country."

"Did he have a good time?"

"Stayed at the reception about five minutes, but I think he enjoyed himself. Took lots of hikes. Borrowed a mountain bike a couple of times from Lang Dillon."

"Is he looking for work?"

"Maybe. He loves books. Works in a bookshop in Boston, but says he's giving up his apartment and coming home for a while. He likes this area much better than Maine. He's got one year left at Northeastern but has taken the year off. Won't tell me why."

"Well, if he's interested, please have him be in touch. We really do need someone, and a book person would be a huge plus."

CHAPTER 3

"This really is a beautiful little village," Richard said as they walked out of the restaurant.

She nodded. "It's pretty special. Thank you for dinner."

"My pleasure. I hope we'll have many more. Care for a walk before we head back?"

"We can walk the boardwalk in whichever direction you'd like."

"You choose."

Lucy pointed southwest, where the land curved past the Fishery and Lab, eventually reaching the point and open sea. "Let's see... The streets are quaint and pretty in that direction, but this way is more scenic, more open space."

"I choose scenic," he said. *Although all the scenery I need is standing next to me.*

"Okay." She turned east to follow the boardwalk that skirted the entire west side of the peninsula.

"This is an incredible feat of engineering," he said. "I've never seen anything quite like it."

"And the upkeep is constant. Every time there's a major storm, it gets washed away, only to be rebuilt."

"So how'd you wind up in Horseshoe Crab Cove anyway?"

"My mom. Well, my parents, actually. They bought a summer

place here. Our mother kept it after the divorce. We've spent our summers here since childhood, but moved here full-time after the divorce."

"Oh?"

"My father was a train wreck. Still is in some ways."

"Does he live nearby?"

"No, he's in Mattapoisett. Bought a condo with his second wife. They moved there a couple of years ago after he sold the family home in New Bedford."

"So did you grow up in New Bedford?"

"Yes. Those were not happy years."

"I'm sorry."

"I have a dark, checkered past. I hope warning bells are sounding for you."

He paused. They'd reached the edge of the village proper, and open fields stretched to their left. "Quite the contrary."

Before she knew what was happening, he pulled her close and kissed her. His lips were warm and soft as they gently opened hers, his tongue tickling. She responded, arms circled his shoulders, lost in the touch and feel of him. Her legs grew shaky, and her body tingled with longing. After ten seconds, she shook herself free and stepped back.

He gave her a warm smile, stroking her arm. "Too much?"

"Yes... No... I don't know," she said.

Deer in the headlights, he mused. "It's okay, sweetheart. I'm sure it's obvious that I'm interested in you and have been since we met in Saguaro."

She smiled shyly. "Yes."

"I've dated a lot of women over the past twenty plus years since my wife died, but never someone like you."

"I'm flattered, Richard. I really am, but I'm just not ready. I had my heart broken by someone I loved very deeply, and I'm still trying to pick up the pieces."

"I can see that, and I won't push you, Lucy. I'd love for us to be friends, though."

"Of course." She gave him a mischievous grin. "But friends don't kiss each other like that."

"Maybe not, but you can't blame a guy for trying."

There it was, the gorgeous Morgan smile that made women from coast to coast go weak at the knees.

"No," she said softly. "Thanks for understanding. Shall we walk a little farther or turn back?"

"Let's go a few minutes more before heading back. I'd love to see what's ahead."

They passed Lolly's mother's estate, a popular destination wedding venue with an enormous house, barns, and cottages. Mavis LaSalle was always booked solid for two years out. Lolly often worked the weddings and sometimes roped her friend in as well. Lucy had served at a number of celebrity weddings over the past ten years. The stars' reps and Mavis herself always swore them to secrecy before and after such events.

As they headed back to town, he took her hand, and they walked in companionable silence. Again, she felt warm and comforted by his touch. Despite the warning bells, she was attracted to the handsome fifty-three-year-old. *And Richard Morgan is hot!*

CHAPTER 4

Wolfie Morgan began working for Lucy and Lolly two weeks before Thanksgiving. A week into his tenure, he moved into Lucy's studio apartment above the garage. An efficient, reliable employee, he was also a considerate, quiet tenant, and Lucy's kids loved having him living at the house. Almost every night when the weather permitted, he and Rob shot baskets in the driveway, and five nights out of seven, Wolfie joined them for dinner. From day one, it was clear Amy had a huge crush on the handsome, dark-eyed, youngest Morgan, with his brown ponytail and quirky ways. "Adonis," Lolly called him, declaring she'd be after him in a heartbeat if she was twenty years younger.

Wolfie also worked at his father's farm some afternoons and on weekends cleaning stalls, helping with mowing and clearing and whatever odd jobs needed doing. As Richard said, Wolfie was a man of few words. Solitary and watchful unless a situation or activity engaged him, he was an enigmatic presence at work and at home. Lucy knew little of his history beyond the fact that his mother had died shortly after his birth. Apparently, she had refused cancer treatment while pregnant with him, treatment that might have saved her life, but would have harmed her unborn child. Lucy had yet to see him with his siblings, three of whom she knew only slightly, the others not at all, but she wondered how he coped in a family of nine.

Late Thursday afternoon, Lolly and Wolfie had departed and Lucy was closing up the office when her cell rang. It was Richard asking her to dinner. "I know it's spur of the moment, but I haven't seen you all week," he said in his rich deep voice.

"I promised to have dinner with the kids, but why don't you join us? Wolfie will be there."

"You've been very good to him. I can't tell you how grateful I am."

"He's delightful, and as I've told you, my two love him. Come. I'm making a huge salad, and I have pizza crusts and fixings. We're all going to create our own."

"Sure you have enough for me?"

"Of course. And we'd be happy to have Weezie or Gail or whoever is over there looking for dinner."

"Thanks, I'll ask, but one never knows about those two. What time?"

"Anytime. I'm headed home now."

"Six?"

"Perfect." She rang off, smiling. It would be interesting to see who showed up. Weezie Morgan had always been friendly, but the few times she'd run into Gail, there had been a distinct icy chill. "She adored her mom and thinks I should be a monk," was Richard's explanation.

RICHARD ARRIVED ON THE DOT OF SIX WITH WEEZIE AND GAIL. AMY greeted them at the door and led them to the kitchen, where Wolfie stood at the counter chopping vegetables. He looked up, surprised to see both sisters. "Hey, the gang's all here," he said. "Lucy's walking the dogs."

"Hi, son," Richard said, grinning. Weezie washed her hands, grabbed a knife, and joined her brother while Gail and her father wandered out to the backyard.

"Nice place," she said.

"Yes. An old family home, I understand."

"Hi, you two," Lucy called, coming round the side yard and unleashing Rufus, their springer spaniel. "I'm sorry I wasn't here to greet you."

Lucy hugged Richard and then turned to Gail, but she stepped back.

"Thanks for having us."

"It's our pleasure. Amy's been really excited. Pizza night is one of her favorites."

"And I'll bet these aren't ordinary pizzas," her father said.

"Can't wait," Gail said, looking as if she was preparing for a root canal.

Lucy wondered why she'd come, but then shrugged it off. "Come on in and get something to drink. What would you like? Wine? Beer? Iced tea? Lemonade? Water? I think we have the gamut, including mixed drinks if you'd like something stronger?"

"Dad brought wine," she said. "I'll have a glass of the white."

Richard frowned at his daughter's rude tone. "And I'll pour! Just point the way to the bar."

Lucy watched the interplay between father and daughter and thought, *yet another reason not to get involved with Richard Morgan.* "Follow me!" she said brightly.

Lucy had perfected the art of making a savory, thin pizza crust, and a stack of crusts sat ready in a basket on the island. Next to this were stone cooking plates, then dozens of bowls with toppings ranging from the traditional to the exotic. Glass of wine in hand, she stood back. "Now this is the fun part. Take a stone and crust, then you can pile on anything you want to make a red or white pizza. I'm a big fan of white pizzas and usually have one with the seafood and cheeses, or a veggie one with the artichoke hearts, mushrooms, onions, and spinach. But, the sky's the limit. When you're all set, all three ovens are heated and ready. They don't take long, so figure eight to ten minutes.

"Once your pizza's in, grab one of the little timers if you need it, then help yourself to salad, find a seat, and relax."

"The perfect hostess," Richard declared, grinning as he grabbed his plate.

Lucy saw Gail's faced cloud over, then she too plunged into the fun of creation.

When everyone sat enjoying his or her pizza, Lucy brought bottles of wine and water to the table and sat down. "Enjoy!"

"This is incredible," Weezie said. "Far and away the best pizza I've ever eaten! How did you make that crust?"

"It's actually really easy," Lucy said. "I'd be happy to show you sometime."

"Isn't there a recipe somewhere?" Gail asked.

"Mom's an amazing cook," Amy said, "but half of what she does, you couldn't write in a recipe. You have to see it, trust me."

"Sounds like a miracle worker," Gail said drolly, receiving a sharp look from her father.

If Amy noticed her tone, she didn't let on. "She is!" she said brightly.

"That she is," Richard said, giving Amy, then Lucy a warm look.

"Thank you," Lucy said. "It's fun. I'm sorry Rob couldn't be here. He'd have enjoyed meeting you all."

Wolfie stood. "Anyone for seconds? I'm going to make another red-and-white pizza for anyone to share, unless you'd like to make your own?"

"Thanks, son, I'm stuffed."

Lucy smiled as Wolfie headed for the kitchen. It was amazing how easily he had fit into their day-to-day routines. Tonight, he seemed to be going out of his way to show his family how much he belonged. *Hmm... I wonder what that's all about?*

They lingered over salad, and each took at least one slice of Wolfie's second round of pizza, despite declaring themselves to be full. As Richard refilled wineglasses, he said, "This is such a festive evening, I think it's a perfect time for a couple of announcements."

His daughters stared at him, mouths agape, but his son, while attentive, seemed calm and relaxed.

"First, I think we may have come up with a name for the new farm."

"Dad!" Gail said, half rising from her seat. "I thought we agreed to wait on that."

"No need, honey. You've already started to spread the word. It's to be called Morgan's Fire, after the incredible sunsets we get almost every night."

"Why didn't anyone tell me?" Weezie said.

"We just decided yesterday, honey, and you were off gallivanting."

Weezie frowned at her sister and father. "But I was home last night and this morning."

Wolfie patted her wrist. "It's done, sis. Let it go. They didn't tell me either."

"Humph!" his sister said. "I can't wait to hear what else I haven't been told."

Her father smiled. "This is a surprise to everyone except Rich."

Gail's face fell, and she wrung her napkin into a tight spiral.

"As some of you may know, the property has an old vineyard at its northeast border. The barn and winery buildings are gone, but the vines are still there. My son Rich got a vintner and a team of viticulturists to come out and take a look."

"When was this?" Gail cried.

"Doesn't matter. They came, they looked things over, and they think there's a good possibility that the vineyard can be revived. It's an ideal location for certain kinds of grapes, according to them. I've talked to Ava and Dan as the biologists in the family," he said, referring to his daughter and her husband. He worked at the Lab in the village that harvested and released the horseshoe crabs, which were plentiful in local waters. Ava was a stay-at-home mom at the moment, but had a master's in environmental science and did occasional jobs at the Lab. It was Dan's job that brought them to the village, and a visit from her dad had started the wheels in motion to move Morgan Enterprises from Maine to Massachusetts.

"I don't believe what I'm hearing," Gail said, hopping up and storming out the back door.

Ignoring her, Richard went on. "I'm hoping Wolfie's degree might come in handy too, if he ever finishes it. Son, I was hoping you might consider taking a role in this."

Wolfie smiled with a slight shake of his head. "You really know how to clear a room, don't you, Dad?"

"What about me?" Weezie asked, who looked for a moment as if she might follow her sister, but then stayed put.

"Baby, there's always going to be a spot for you in whatever venture you'd like to be a part of."

"Except not a leadership role?"

"Someday."

Lucy began to clear the plates, feeling as if she and Amy were intruding on what was clearly a Morgan family discussion. "Anyone for ice cream or coffee?" she asked as she stood, holding a stack of plates.

CHAPTER 5

"Sorry about that," he said as Lucy scooped ice cream into bowls. "I'm confused as to why you did it tonight, here."

"I wanted a buffer. And I wanted my son to be in a place he feels comfortable, which he clearly does here. I want Wolfie to run the vineyard, if he wants to. Had I brought this up amongst his siblings, he'd have headed for the hills, never to be seen again."

"Is this what he wants?"

"The boy doesn't know what he wants, but he's smart. If he ever graduates, he'll have a bioengineering degree, which might be useful."

Lucy stopped what she was doing and met his eyes. She glimpsed fire, yet also sadness in their dark depths. She reached out and touched his arm. "It's been my experience that people rarely like to be told what they want to do by someone else, especially a parent."

He placed his hands on her waist and drew her nearer. "See how much I need you in my life? I need someone to talk sense to me."

She smiled. "I doubt that." *He really is a gorgeous man, so different from Rob,* she thought. Her almost ex-husband was her age, a runner, lean and toned. Tall and slender, Richard was grounded and confident in a way Rob had never been. Richard knew what he wanted and went after it. At the moment, his hands were sending waves of warmth from her head to her toes.

He grinned. "I s'pose kissing you now would be a no-no."

"A big one." She gently removed his hands and turned back to her task. "Now why don't you deliver these and see if you can find Gail."

"Let her stew," he said, then picked up two bowls and headed for the dining room.

"I've never had this flavor," Weezie said, waving her spoon. "It's delicious. What is it?"

"Swiss orange chocolate chip. It's Mom's favorite," Amy said.

Lucy smiled at her cohostess. "She's right. I'm addicted, and it's hard to find. Cove Creamery and Sullivan's in Tucson are the only places I've ever found this flavor."

"Did you go to Tucson when you were out west?"

"Day trip. My mom and Leonora went museum hopping and ate lunch at Sullivan's. They have the best burgers, and the ice cream is to die for."

So are you, Richard mused, watching her. *You have no idea how beautiful you are Lucy Brennan.*

Lucy excused herself and went in search of Gail, who she found swinging on the backyard glider. "Want some ice cream?"

"No thanks." She looked away.

"Coffee?"

"Thanks, but I'm just gonna hang out here till the others are ready to leave."

"Want some company?"

"Not especially, but thanks for asking. This is our dad. Everyone's welcome till they're not. He's all business and I'm obviously not in his inner circle."

"Sometimes it's helpful to tease out ideas with a couple of people before widening the circle," Lucy said. "Then you don't confuse or disappoint the people you care about most."

"Is that the way you conduct business?"

Lucy smiled. "No, but I'm small potatoes compared to your dad. It's just my partner and me in a cubbyhole office in the village."

"And our brother."

"Yes."

Lucy studied Richard's auburn-haired daughter. Her curly hair was shoulder length, the scruffy pageboy not particularly flattering in Lucy's opinion. Petite with hazel eyes and freckles, she wore clothes that did little to enhance her appearance. In contrast to her dark-haired siblings, Gail seemed plain and dull, but Lucy suspected there was beauty hidden underneath the baggy sweaters and ill-fitting khakis.

She'd seen the oldest, Rich, a few times around the village. He was fair-haired, handsome, and always well-dressed. Lovely Ava, the biologist, was an earth mother with long chestnut hair, a full figure, and a smile like her dad's. Lucy often encountered Ava and her husband, Dan, hiking on the trails around the village, their three young children in backpacks and jogging strollers.

"Wolfie's lucky. He escaped."

"And you can't?"

Gail shook her head and stood. "I've gotta get home." Without a word, she brushed past Lucy and went into the house.

For a minute, Lucy stood watching her. *Did I touch a nerve?*

When they got inside, they found that Wolfie had excused himself and retreated to his apartment and Amy to her room to do homework. "There you are," Richard said to his daughter.

"Can we go now?" she said. "I've got things to do tonight."

"Of course. You ready, Weez?"

"Why not? Thanks for a great dinner, Lucy. Say bye to Amy for me, will you?"

Lucy smiled, hugging her. "Will do."

Halfway out the door, Gail turned and mumbled, "Yeah, thanks," before disappearing.

Richard shook his head. "Sorry, she's my prickly girl. I've always called her Mrs. Tiggy-Winkle after that Beatrix Potter book about the hedgehog."

Lucy laughed. "No worries."

Richard turned to his other daughter. "You go out with Gail, honey. I'll just be a minute."

On her way out the door, Weezie winked at her and said, "Thanks again!"

Richard closed the door behind his daughter leaving her and Lucy alone. He drew her into his arms. "This was really nice of you. Would it be too bold if I stole a chaste kiss?"

In answer, she slid arms around his shoulders and kissed him softly. He responded, and the kiss deepened, tongues twining and teasing in a sensuous dance, his hands moving up and down her back. As her knees began to tremble, she broke away.

Bushy eyebrows arched mischievously, his eyes lit up, he said, "That was nice."

"Yes, it was." She ran her fingers along his strong jaw. "Now you'd better scoot."

"You know you've just given me a shot of encouragement."

"Good night," she said, opening the door and waving him out. As she closed the door, Lucy broke out into a huge grin. *Richard Morgan is a wonderful kisser!*

CHAPTER 6

Daydreaming about Lucy's soft, peach skin, Richard waited in the Crab Café for his nephew, Kyle. He didn't know how he was going to woo her, but every time he saw her, he became more determined.

"Hey, Uncle Dick," startled him out of his reverie.

"Mornin', my good doc. Thanks for comin'. I hear through the grapevine that you're in high demand."

Kyle grinned, sliding into the booth opposite him, bagel in hand. "Sorry, do you want something?"

"No, thanks, just ate. So you're busy, huh?"

"People around here love their pets, and they have lots of 'em."

"Well, before we get down to the business of my pets and how much time you have for them, I hope you and Harriet are planning to come for Thanksgiving. I asked Lucy and her kids, but apparently, the kids go with their dad. I told her to ask your mother-in-law and her sisters too."

"I think Harriet mentioned something about it this morning, so count us in. We'll want to bring something."

"Just yourselves, son. My cook, Callie, does everything."

"So what's going on out at the farm? I haven't been out since I checked on Crackers."

"Everything's great. Rich told you about the vineyard, right?"

"Sure did. Cool."

"We had a vineyard in Maine. It's fun. Still going strong with the new owners. I miss it. It'll be three to five years before we get a decent harvest, but you gotta start somewhere, right? The vines are there, but they need a lot of TLC to bring them back."

"And you guys are the ones to do it."

"Along with our vintner and his crew. So Dr. Morgan, what I wanted to discuss with you is regular veterinary services once the farm's up and running. You in?"

"I'm happy to assist, Uncle Dick, but it would be my recommendation that if you gear up to an operation like Dad's and Spark's, you should consider hiring a resident vet."

"The job's yours, if you want it."

"Thanks. I really appreciate your confidence, but I've kind of made a commitment to the practice in town. And, truth be told, I really like it. Don't get me wrong, I love the horses, but I've really enjoyed having kids come in with their puppies, hamsters, bunnies, whatever. I'd hate to give that up, especially as I'm the village's only vet. I'm happy to act as a consultant, though."

"Would you help us find a good doc? Sit in on interviews?"

"Of course. You know, I could reach out to some of my fellow vet school students. They're all over the country now, but I've kept in touch with our cohort. Want me to shoot them an email?"

"That'd be terrific, son. Does Rich have your email?"

Kyle nodded. "We're in touch all the time about pickup basketball games."

"Great. I'll tell him to email you the job description."

"Speak of the devil," Kyle said, looking past his uncle's head. "Hey, Rich."

"Mornin'," Rich said, nodding at Kyle. "Dad, I've been calling you."

"Phone's switched off. Important meeting."

"We've had some news."

"Well, sit down and cough it up. Anything you have to say to me, you can say to our consulting doc."

Rich hesitated, then sat beside his father. "I had a call from Gus this morning."

"Oh? Is he considering our offer to come back for a month or so?"

Rich grinned. "Good thing you're sitting. No, he called to see if the position of head trainer and director of the rescue program was still available."

"Why, does he know someone?"

"Him."

His father stared at him openmouthed. "Excuse me?"

"They want to move back east. Lynn's mom is ill, and she wants to be nearer to Connecticut."

"When?"

"As soon as they can find a replacement at the Cottage and Gus's replacement at Valley Stables. He says they've got a line on someone for his job and they've got feelers out for Lynn's."

"My brother and Spark must be shitting bullets."

"They're sad to lose him, but they understand. It's not like we're trying to poach Gus. Actually, Leonora's more upset about losing Lynn as Cottage codirector, but she is, of course, compassionate and accepting about her need to be closer to home. They thought about living in Connecticut, but then figured this is close enough for Lynn to go back and forth. They'd like to move and get settled before the baby comes."

Richard whistled. "Geez, Louise! You just made my day. Let's sit down this afternoon and make up a package for him."

CHAPTER 7

"You've got to come with me," Lolly said. "Both of you! I can't do this alone."

"If Marla's playing, won't your friends and family be there?" Lucy asked, referring to Lolly's younger sister who was part of a folk band, the Cherry Pickers. The group was playing at Sandy's, Lolly's ex-husband's club.

"Think of how many times we've been to Sandy's over the years."

"Not since the unmentionable and I split up."

"It'll be so jammed, you probably won't even run into him."

"Ha-ha, nice try. You're coming. You too, Wolfie."

"Folk's not really my thing."

Lolly handed him a stack of books, a flyer for the event on top. "Well, it's next Saturday, and you're coming or you're fired."

"No, you're not," Lucy said. "Of course I'll go and drag Amy. Not sure about Rob." She looked at Wolfie. "Does your dad like folk music?"

"Loves it."

"So we can ask him. Maybe Weezie and Gail? That'll give you plenty of buffers. Is Maisie coming?"

"For a while. Mom's coming with Thad, her latest boyfriend. I even heard that dear old Dad's making the trip. I hope he doesn't bring any of those actors' studio hangers-on." Lolly's father was a Broadway producer and always had a new lady friend, many of them younger than his daughters.

"I'm in," Wolfie said. "Not for fear of losing my job, but I'm all for solidarity."

Lolly smiled at their handsome, dark-haired assistant. "You are a peach, Wolfie Morgan. Maybe I'll even pretend that you're my date."

He gave her a wry smile.

"Too much?" Lolly said.

"Maybe a little. I suppose it'd be okay if we walked in arm in arm."

"I would hug you, but I don't want to be slapped with a harassment suit."

"Okay, it's settled. Now can we get back to work?" Lucy asked, noticing that piles of books were being passed and sorted willy-nilly. "Remember, we've only got three days till the fair." The village harvest fair was happening Saturday, and they always had a large book table. This year was no exception. It was a huge fair, attended by people throughout New England and beyond.

"Mom's expecting our illustrious authors Friday night," Lolly said.

Each year, they invited one or two children's writers to sign books at the fair. This year, they had popular picture book artist Dale Weiz and young adult novelist Karen Platt. Both were hot and much in demand. Weiz had won the Caldecott the previous year and Platt two Newberys.

"Where's she putting them?"

"Netherfield. She offered them one of the cottages, but they wanted to be nearer the spa and workout rooms."

"The table's gonna be mobbed. Teenagers are crazy about Karen, and, as we know, Dale's a true publishing sensation the likes of which we're not likely to see again."

"How did you get them to come to little ole Horseshoe Crab Cove?" Wolfie asked.

"Our company helps keep them in business, and they know it. We have a huge mailing list. We sell as many books as some of the chains," Lolly said.

"Doesn't hurt that both are fairly local and the fair attracts a lot of people including publishers, librarians, and tons of book people," Lucy said. "Listen, guys, I've gotta run. Your dad's taking me to Ballard's for dinner."

"Ooh, lah lah!" Lolly said. "Must be serious."

"What's Ballard's?" he asked.

"A fancy schmancy seafood restaurant up the coast in the snooty town of Leeside. Food's to die for," Lolly said.

"It's not *that* fancy," Lucy said, grabbing her bag. "See you!"

"SO, WE'VE GOT A PACKAGE WE'RE SENDING TO GUS TONIGHT," RICHARD said, Weezie, Gail and Rich sitting with him at the dining room table. "I was hoping to have ideas for a job for Lynn and a caregiver for the baby, but with the salary I'm paying him, she doesn't have to work. We'll see. One step at a time."

"What about Kyle's wife? She works at a school," Weezie said.

Her father shook his head. "It's a boarding school, and I don't think it has a preschool."

Gail slumped in her chair, yawning. "There've got to be nursery schools in the area."

"She's been a director out there and makes a salary they couldn't possibly match around here," her brother said.

Gail frowned. "So, are they demanding you find something for her, then?"

Richard gave her a sharp look. "No, I'm just trying to be helpful."

Rich looked around the table, then spoke to his father. "I'll send this off and put out some feelers in the village. What about Lucy? Would she know of anything?"

"I'll certainly ask her. We're having dinner tonight, which reminds me, I've got to end this meeting soon."

"Again?" Gail said.

Richard stared at her, a confused look on his face. "Excuse me? We've pretty much covered today's agenda, haven't we?"

"I'm talking about your date."

"Leave it alone, sis," Rich said.

"I like her!" Weezie said brightly. "And I like her kids too. I don't blame Wolfie one bit for moving over there to get away from Ms. Gloom and Doom here."

Richard waved his hands. "That's enough. The frequency of my engagements with Lucy are my business, and speculating on your brother's motives is nonsense. As you well know, Wolfie has always preferred to be independent."

Rich stood. "Meeting adjourned. Dad, have fun tonight. I'm off to soccer."

"Is that a coed league?" Weezie asked, referring to the pickup games her brother joined once or twice a week.

"Yes, but I thought you were joining the polo club in Richmond?"

"Can't I do both?"

"Thursdays, five to seven, community fields behind the Town Hall."

Rich and Weezie disappeared, leaving the others at the table. Richard gazed at his prickly child, who was shuffling papers, a pout on her face. "Hey, princess, what's wrong?"

"Don't call me that! I'm not five anymore."

"Gail, talk to me."

"It's nothing. I'm fine."

"You don't seem fine, and you haven't for a while. Are you sure this is what you want?"

"Dad, we've had this conversation a hundred times. I like living here, and I love working for the company."

"But you don't seem to have much of a life, sweetheart. That's what worries me. I wish you'd get out and meet some friends."

"They're all in Maine, remember?"

"So find some new ones! Join the gym. There's also that fancy spa that Lucy's partner's mom runs. They have memberships. Or what about a hiking club or—"

Gail put up her hands, "Dad, stop! I'm okay. Really." She pushed back her chair and stormed from the room.

Richard shook his head. *She's twenty-six years old. You can't fix her life. Only she can do that.*

CHAPTER 8

Lucy chose one of her favorite dresses, a soft green cashmere that draped beautifully and hugged her slender figure. It needed no adornment, but she decided upon a mother-of-pearl beaded necklace and matching earrings that picked up the soft blue of her eyes. She slipped into beige heels that she knew flattered her slender legs and gazed in the mirror. "Not bad," she said aloud. Finally, she brushed her hair back, leaving it loose.

Her care was rewarded when she opened the door and saw Richard's face.

"Wow! You look sensational!"

She made a mock curtsey. "Thanks. So do you." And he did, in a charcoal-gray sport jacket, tan shirt, and dark brown tie. Lucy had worked in a high-end men's shop during college. Perfectly tailored and pressed, Richard's clothes probably cost more than Merlin's Closet made in a month.

"One of the perks of wealth," he said. "A tailor."

"Oh my. Did you bring him from Maine?"

He laughed. "No, he's in London, actually. Met him when we lived in Singapore and have followed him around the globe. Wherever he is, I visit him once or twice a year. Now that I'm a farmer, a visit to

Max every few years will probably be all that's needed to keep me spruced up enough to escort a beautiful woman to dinner. Shall we?"

A *different world*, Lucy thought, taking his hand.

BALLARD'S, A POPULAR, LONG-ESTABLISHED RESTAURANT WITH A WORLD-class chef, was Lucy's favorite restaurant in the area. No sooner had she shared that with Richard than he had proposed they have this dinner. Now, here they were, gazing out at the ocean, their table one of the best in the house.

"If the food's half as good as this view, I'll be a happy man."

"Yes, it's a beautiful spot," she said, looking out at the waves crashing over the rocks below.

"I wasn't talking about the ocean view," he said, smiling as he took her hand.

Lucy sat up, but left her hand in his. "I don't know how you got this table, but it's lovely."

"That's my little secret," he said, "But you're lovely too."

"Thank you." She blushed just as the waiter appeared.

"Hello and welcome to Ballard's. I'm Jamie. I'll be serving you tonight. Can I start you off with a cocktail?"

Richard looked at her. "Wine?"

"Yes, white, please."

He studied the wine list briefly, ordered a bottle, and Jamie disappeared.

"So. What were we discussing?"

"Nothing," she said.

"Oh, I remember. We were discussing your great beauty."

"And I believe we have exhausted that subject. What's new over at Morgan's Fire? I love the name, by the way."

"Me too. Well...hmm... We may have our head trainer and manager. Fingers crossed. The offer went out to him today."

"Congratulations. Is he from this area?"

"Saguaro Valley."

"What?"

He grinned. "Gus Casey."

"But how can you do that to your brother and Spark? Won't they be terribly upset?"

"It's Gus's decision. They want to move east because Lynn's mother is ill."

"Oh, I'm sorry to hear that."

"Yes, very sudden. Doesn't sound good."

"Well, I'm happy for you."

Jamie returned with the wine, and after pouring it, he explained the specials. "I'll give you a few minutes and pop back, shall I?"

Richard nodded. "Thanks, son." As Jamie moved away, he said. "What are you thinking?"

"Well, I love bouillabaisse and I really like the way they make it. You?"

"The swordfish special sounded great. I haven't had it in a few months, so I think I'm safe."

They chatted about the farm for a few minutes before he said, "Lucy, I'm so grateful to you for taking Wolfie in and under your wing."

"It's been a pleasure. Amy and Rob adore him, and he's been a tremendous help to Lolly and me."

"I'm glad. He seems happier than I've seen him in a long while."

"That reminds me. We're all going to Sandy's, a club not far from here Saturday night to see Lolly's sister's band, the Cherry Pickers. Wolfie has agreed to accompany us. It's folk music. Would you be interested in joining us?"

He clapped his hands. "I'd love to!"

Lucy smiled. There was such genuine joy and kindness in the man sitting across from her. Like a kid in a candy store, he embraced life, and his excitement was infectious. "It's casual."

"I know Sandy's," he said. "The owner's an old friend."

"Sandy Rodriguez is a friend of yours?"

"Maybe more of an acquaintance. He came up to Maine and

worked for us one summer when he was in college. Good kid. My Ava had a huge crush on him."

"Oh my goodness. What a small world. Is she his age?"

"Nope. Much younger. She was barely in high school when heartthrob Sandy stole her heart."

"He's my partner's ex."

"Really?"

"And it's an acrimonious situation."

"Hmm... Is she attending the concert?"

"Yes, but that's why we're all going. Reinforcements or maybe buffers. She's thinking of pretending Wolfie's her date."

He laughed. "Well, I promise not to spend much time consorting with the enemy."

"It's fine. Sandy's a great guy. Monogamy isn't for him, I guess. He broke Lolly's heart."

AFTER RICHARD SETTLED THE CHECK, HE SUGGESTED THEY HAVE A nightcap in the bar. "I'd invite you back to my place, but that wouldn't be very romantic," he said.

"Mine either," she said as she sipped the smooth, delicious brandy he'd ordered.

"What will we do about this?"

"Nothing," she said, reaching over to squeeze his hand. "I really enjoy your company, Richard. I do. I'm just not ready for more right now."

"I know, but you can't blame a guy for fantasizing, can you?"

She smiled. "No."

When they got to the car, he opened her door, and she turned to him. The wine and brandy had made her slightly tipsy, and his closeness warmed her. "You are a wonderful man, Richard Morgan," she said, draping her arms over his shoulders.

He kissed her forehead. "What happened to not ready?"

"One little kiss couldn't hurt, could it?"

In answer, he swept her into his arms and kissed her long and deep. Lucy's knees buckled as she gave herself to him, her fingers caressing his neck as his hands moved up and down her body, grazing her breasts. She could feel him grow hard, and she pressed herself closer, gently rocking and swaying.

Breathless, he whispered, "Should we find a room? Either that or I might ravish you right here on the clamshell parking lot."

She laughed, stepping back. "I'm sorry. I don't know what came over me."

"Well, whatever it was, I want more."

"I know, but not tonight. We'd better go."

"Party pooper," he said, kissing her lightly.

I'm really going to have to decide about this, Lucy thought after saying good night at her door. Her body ached for his at the same time her heart screamed *no*.

CHAPTER 9

"Make an appointment with Elise," Harriet said as the two sisters sat in Lucy's kitchen eating bagels and catching up. Lucy had been describing her warring emotions in relation to Richard. "He seems like a great guy. Kyle loves him and is really excited about the stables."

"He's his uncle. Of course he loves him. And I'm very fond of him and *very* attracted to him. That's not the issue. After Rob, I just feel like I need more healing time. If I jump into something with Richard, I'm afraid I'll screw it up."

Harriet met her eyes. "Lucy, you did nothing to screw up your marriage. Rob did that all by himself."

Her sister shrugged. "Maybe, but he obviously got bored. Maybe between the kids and the business, I neglected him?"

"Do you hear yourself? This is why you need to talk to Elise!"

"Maybe. He is a nice man, isn't he?"

Harriet nodded. "Kyle calls him Uncle Dick."

"I know, but I've always called him Richard. I asked which he prefers, and he says he likes the fact that I have a special name for him."

"Aw, that's so sweet. Where are my niece and nephew anyway?"

"Amy slept at Meghan's house, and Rob's at his dad's."

"Shoot. I haven't seen 'em in forever. You guys'll have to come to dinner soon. Are they coming to Thanksgiving at the farm?"

"No, Thanksgiving's Rob's holiday this year. I have them Christmas, then he's taking them on a New Year's cruise."

"Well, then dinner next week."

"We're all going to Sandy's tonight to see Lolly's sister Marla's band. Wanta come?"

"That sounds fun. How will that be for Lolly?"

"Who knows, but we're all going to surround her so she'll be invisible to the unmentionable."

"Fat chance of that. I'll ask Kyle. Are you eating there?"

"Probably."

"What time?"

"Sevenish."

"Sounds good. I'll give you a call after I talk to Kyle. Gotta run," Harriet said, standing and grabbing her bag. "I hope the fair goes well."

"You're not coming?"

"I'm taking Mom to Providence, remember? We'll stop on our way back."

"Okay. Maybe I'll see you later."

As Harriet disappeared, Lucy fingered the slip of paper with Elise Nolan's number. *What the hell*, she thought, grabbing her phone. She called and left a message asking for an appointment the following week.

"This is nice," Richard said, holding her close as the band played Donovan's "Catch the Wind."

"And this is one of my favorite folk songs," Lucy said, resting her head on his shoulder. Exhausted after spending the day at the book fair, she wondered if she could stay awake.

"I'm completely happy right now," he whispered.

"Me too," she said, tears rimming her eyes as they gazed up to meet his.

"Hey, none of that," he said, kissing her forehead. "This moment is special, that's all."

Sandy's was packed, but not packed enough that Lolly and Amy didn't see the exchange from where they sat. "He's in love with her, isn't he, Aunt Lolly?"

"Yup."

"What do you think about Mom? Does she feel the same way?"

"I'd say yes, but she's not ready to admit it. Not quite ready to take the plunge."

"Do you blame her?"

"Nope." Lolly's attention was no longer on her friend, but the side of the stage where Sandy Rodriguez stood talking to two men. A blonde twenty-something woman hung on to his arm.

The next song was a fast one, "Build Me Up Buttercup," and Lolly hopped up, dragging Wolfie out onto the dance floor. "Come on, Buttercup, they're playing our song."

"What a contrast," Richard said, laughing as the song started. "And not exactly a folk song."

"The Cherry Pickers are kind of eclectic." Lucy took his arm. "Let's get some air or something to drink."

"I vote for air," he said.

As they passed by their table, Amy gave her a thumbs-up, then turned to greet her friends who had just arrived.

"Looks like Amy's okay and Lolly's commandeered Wolfie, so we're free."

"Yes," he said, opening the slider at the end of the cavernous room. She slipped out, and he shut the door behind them.

"Ooh, it's colder than I thought," she said, rubbing her arms.

"Want me to get your jacket?"

"No, I'm fine."

"Here," he said, pulling his sweater over his head. "Put this on."

"Then you'll be cold."

"Beside you? Never."

She put up her arms as he slipped it over her head. "Thanks. We won't stay out long."

"Just long enough for this?" he pulled her into his arms and kissed her deeply, tongue laced around hers, his yearning raw and urgent.

Lucy responded, her arms circling his shoulders. In that moment she decided to give herself to him. As he grew hard, she began a rhythmic rubbing, her hips pressed against him.

"Are you trying to kill me, my love?" he said hoarsely. "Much more of this and I'll have to brave the cold and ravish you right here."

Lucy pulled him into the shadows of the club's back porch. Sheltered from the wind, it was warmer and completely hidden. "Go ahead," she whispered, kissing his neck, stroking him below the belt until he groaned with pleasure.

"Are you serious?"

In answer, she slipped off her jeans and panties and threw them to the side. "Yes, very serious." She reached down and unzipped his jeans, releasing him, then stroking, caressing.

Richard whispered. "I haven't got protection."

"I do," she lied. "I do."

"That's my girl," he whispered, leaning back against the wall, lifting her legs, wrapping them around him. "Ready?"

She nodded as her hand guided him between her legs, her moist depths beckoning. He pulled her down on him, and she cried out, "Oh!"

"Too much?"

"No, more, more, more," she murmured, awed by the size of him, warmed and comforted at how well they fit.

As their bodies moved in tandem, the cold forgotten, they thrust again and again, unable to get enough of each other. Finally, he released just as Lucy's explosive orgasm crested and she collapsed, limp and sated in his arms.

"Anyone out here?" a voice called from the darkness.

"Jesus," Richard whispered, setting her down, shielding her with his body. "Give us a minute, would you, pal?" he called. A door closed, and they were alone again.

Lucy scrambled to find her clothes, pulling on panties and jeans, searching in the darkness for her loafers. Finally back together, she slipped off his sweater and handed it to him. "Thanks, I'm warm now."

"We'd better get back inside before they send a search party," he said, drawing her close. "But I'd rather stay here all night with you, sweet girl."

She nuzzled his shoulder, then kissed him softly. "Me too."

As they made their way through the crowd, Lucy suddenly felt faint as the realization of what they'd just done washed over her. It was at that moment that Rob tapped her on the shoulder.

CHAPTER 10

"It is you. I thought so," her ex-husband said. "Great music, huh?"

Lucy's face reddened, and she stammered, "Oh, hello... Yes." Richard stood at her side, peering from one to the other.

Shaking herself, she said, "This is Richard. Richard, Rob Brennan."

The men shook hands. Richard grinned. "So this is Dr. Brennan. I just made an appointment with one of your associates."

Rob nodded, then turned back to her. "How are you?"

"Fine."

"Are the kids here?"

"Just Amy." Lucy pointed to a table in the far corner where Amy and her friends now sat. Lolly and Wolfie were on the dance floor.

"Hey, Robbie, this is one of my favorites!" said a voice said behind him. A tall, anorexically thin blonde appeared at his side. When she spied Lucy, she frowned. "Oh, it's you." She turned to Richard, extending her hand. "Chloe Birdsong."

"Richard Morgan, new to town."

"You're not the Morgan who's developing that huge farm north of town, are you?"

"Guilty as charged."

"I love horses," she said.

"Well, we're gonna have a bunch," he said, feeling Lucy's discomfort beside him. "Great band."

"Yeah, come on, Robbie, let's go," Chloe whined, pulling his arm.

Rob shrugged, looking vaguely embarrassed. "I guess we're going to dance. See you." He turned to Richard. "Good to meet you. I'm sure I'll see you around town."

As they walked off, Lucy said, "Excuse me, would you? Going to the ladies' room." She hurried off without waiting for his response.

When she pushed open the door, she turned to find Lolly right behind her. "Not now," she said, rushing to a stall and vomiting.

"Hey, sweetie, you okay?" Lolly said. "We're the only ones in here."

No response.

"Want a wet towel?"

"No, I'll be out in a minute."

When she emerged, her eyes were red and her cheeks blotchy. Lolly hugged her for a long time. "Hey, it's okay. We've all been there. It sucks."

Lucy sniffed. "I don't even know why I'm crying. I just had incredible sex with an amazing man who cares about me."

"Oh my God, you had sex? Where?"

"On the deck. Maybe it was a bad margarita?"

"Maybe. Or maybe after your incredible sex on the deck, seeing your ex and his bimbo made you sick? Talk about highs and lows."

"God, what a basket case I am. This is why I shouldn't be starting a relationship. I'm a huge mess. What must Richard be thinking?"

"He's fine. Kyle and your sister just got here, so he's having a grand ole time. Amy and her friends love him too."

"I need help, don't I?"

"You need to move on and let go of Rob Brennan. He's an asshole, and so is she. What kind of crazy people pay good money for nutritional advice from a swizzle stick?"

"That's exactly what I need to do. Let go. Everything seems so strange right now. *That* was my life and this is—"

"A new season, as Elise keeps telling me."

"You like her, huh?"

"Love her, even though I'm having the same issue—letting go, accepting, moving on. It sucks."

"It totally sucks," Lucy said, patting her friend's arm. "Let's go out and show 'em we've moved on. I have a good mind to ask Marla if the band can play 'Something to Talk About.'"

"I love it! Let's do it!"

"Thanks, partner."

"Seeing you and Lolly dancing out there was worth the price of admission," Richard said as they pulled into the driveway. Amy had stayed, saying she'd hitch a ride with Harriet and Kyle.

"I don't know about that, but it helped change the mood."

He turned off the car and reached over to take her hand. "Was that too much? Did I... Did what we... I'm sorry if—"

"No. That...out on the deck was amazing. I think I may have had too much to drink, and then seeing Rob... It's still hard when it's unexpected, you know? The unknown, the unpredictable...leftover baggage. The aftermath of knowing your husband was doing something for over a year that would shatter your life and you never knew. It's creepy and unsettling and a host of other things."

"I'm sorry. I can't imagine."

"You are a wonderful man, Richard Morgan. I'm still trying to figure life out, and I think I need to talk to someone. There's a great therapist in the village."

"I'm a big fan of therapy. Saved my life more than once."

As they walked arm in arm to the door, she leaned her head on his shoulder. "Thanks for being patient with me."

"You'll figure things out, sweetheart. Just takes time." He kissed her lightly and said, "You gonna be okay?"

"Yes, I'm going straight to bed. If I know my sister, Amy'll be home soon. Night."

She stood in the light of the doorway, waving as he drove off. *I sure hope I figure things out, because he is a wonderful man.*

CHAPTER 11

Sunday morning, Lucy picked up Helen, and they headed to Hampton Meeting where they attended Meeting for Worship at least once or twice a month. Today, they sat with Harriet and Kyle. It was a quiet meeting, with very few people moved to speak. Aside from listening to the opening prayer and a few announcements, Lucy's mind roamed to the past few weeks and the previous night especially.

A turning point in their relationship, for sure, and one she'd been avoiding for fear of getting in too deep too fast. Now that she'd experienced it, she wanted more, much more. Richard was an amazing kisser, his lips soft, just the right play of tongue. She could still feel his strong, farmer's hands grasping her ass and the size of his cock that filled her so completely. Suddenly noticing her lascivious thoughts, she shook herself. *This is Meeting for Worship, you wanton woman!*

They went to brunch at the Maple Crossing, a small mom-and-pop restaurant near the campus of Hampton Meeting School, where Harriet taught and she and Kyle now lived in one of the school cottages. Over thick French toast and crisp local bacon, they shared their weeks. Helen sat quietly listening.

"Gonna be great having Gus at Morgan's Fire," Kyle said. "Uncle Dick is over the moon."

Harriet smiled at her handsome husband, who always looked like a kid on Christmas morning. "I keep meaning to ask. Where did they come up with the name Morgan's Fire?"

"It was inspired by the incredible sunsets they get, but it's actually going to be their wine label when the vineyard starts producing. I think they figured why not brand the whole place? Good advance PR for the winery and the thoroughbred operation."

Harriet shook her head. "It's almost like they're recreating Saguaro Valley, only on steroids."

"That's Uncle Dick," Kyle said. "He seems to thrive on having many irons in the fire. Morgan Enterprises has all kinds of businesses all over the place. Excuse me, ladies." He rose and went to pay the bill, immediately caught up in a conversation with two locals near the cash register.

Helen smiled, sipping her tea. "Like a couple of other men we know out west. Have you decided about going west for Christmas?"

Harriet nodded. "We have. We're going. I'm sure Spark would be happy to have you as well. I think the plan is for us to stay at Beth and Lang's, so there'd also be room at the Big House or Harley and Ruthie's."

"Sounds lovely, my dear, but I think I'll stay put. I have a small window commission to complete and lots of house projects," Helen said.

"And she'll be with us. Hazel, Clara, and Will are coming. This may be my last Christmas in the house. Maybe one more, but after the divorce goes through, I'm going to think about next steps. No sense hanging on."

"Does this have anything to do with your handsome gentleman farmer?" her sister asked, a twinkle in her eye.

"No...not necessarily, but he's an example of me taking next steps, no matter where they take me."

Harriet twirled a bite of French toast on her fork. "Maybe to that gorgeous farmhouse on Morgan's Fire?"

Lucy smiled. "That's *really* getting ahead of things."

"I can't wait to see how they're going to fit us all this Thursday," Harriet said. "They must have a mile-long table."

"How many?" Helen asked.

"I think he said around twenty. There's us, all eight of his kids, grandkids, spouses, girlfriends, and I think Dennis Farrell and maybe another worker or two."

"Wow," Harriet said. "Even though I'll miss 'em, I guess it's good that Amy and Rob will be with their dad. Are they at his house?"

"His sister's," Lucy replied, recalling a chilly encounter she'd had a week earlier with Sally Brennan Miller, her sister-in-law. They'd never been best friends, but she and Sally had enjoyed watching their children grow up and collaborating on family celebrations. She missed the Brennan holidays.

They'd run into each other outside the Crab Café, Sally laden with takeout bags. She worked as a receptionist in her brother's medical practice. Surprised, Lucy had said, "Hello, Sally! So good to see you."

"Hungry hoards waiting, can't stop to chat," her sister-in-law had replied. "Hope you have a good holiday. We're so looking forward to spending it with Amy and Rob. Ta-ta!"

Lucy had stood on the sidewalk for several minutes watching Sally walk toward the office before turning away and heading into the Café. *Life turns on a dime*, she mused.

"Sis? You okay?" Harriet asked, interrupting her reverie.

Lucy smiled. "Fine."

Later, as she dropped her mother off, Helen turned to her. "Want to come in?"

"Thanks, Mum, but I've got a lot to do." She leaned over and kissed Helen's cheek.

"Are you okay? Really okay?"

"Yup, just lots of transitions. Everything seems new, nothing familiar, you know?"

Helen nodded. "It gets better. You're in a new season now, and you'll find new familiar, comforting rituals and routines."

"Thanks, Mum. Shall I pick you up Thursday morning?"

"Harriet offered. We could come and get you too."

"I'll give her a call. Have a lovely afternoon."

As she drove away from Helen's beautiful shingled cottage surrounded by fields and dunes, she thought about the painful journey that had brought her mother to this peaceful, beloved home. *If she can do it, so can I!*

HER CELL PHONE BUZZED AS SHE DROVE INTO THE DRIVEWAY. LUCY parked and fished it out of her purse. She wasn't surprised to see her attorney Chris D'Angelo's name. "Hi, Chris," she said, turning off the ignition.

There was a slight pause, then he said, "Hi, Lucy. How you doing?"

"Pretty good."

"You ready for tomorrow?"

"As ready as I'll ever be."

"Anyone coming with you?"

"Just you. That's enough. Harriet and Lolly offered, but I'll be fine. It's going to be quick, right?"

"As quick as I can make it. We should be one of the first cases up."

"Okay."

"Lucy, it's going to be all right. This is the last step, then you're free."

"Yes."

"Meet you inside the courthouse at eight forty-five?"

"I'll be there."

After they rang off, she walked up on the porch, sat in one of the rockers, and shut her eyes. *How can this be happening to me? What happened to the life I knew and loved so dearly?*

Fifteen minutes later, she was still sitting, eyes closed, when someone stepped onto the porch. "Hey, Lucy."

"Rob!" Her eyes popped open to find her almost ex-husband standing over her, looking relaxed and handsome in jeans and a sweatshirt. "What are you doing here?"

"I wanted to check in. Seeing you last night... I just thought I'd see if you were okay."

"Why wouldn't I be?"

"Well, tomorrow's court, and I was with Chloe last night."

Lucy rubbed her arms, a sudden breeze chilling her. "And?"

"Sally said she ran into you last week."

"Yes."

"How was that?"

"Rob, is there something you want?"

"I care about you, Luce. I just wanted to make sure you're okay."

She stood, arms splayed. "First of all, you don't get to call me Luce anymore. Second, you have no right to come by unannounced unless you're picking up the kids, neither of whom are here."

"Okay."

Hands on hips, she faced him. *Stay strong, girl, stay strong!* "Is there anything else?"

"No, I guess not. See you tomorrow, then?"

"Yes."

"Want a ride to the courthouse?"

"To get our divorce? No, I don't think so."

"Okay, then."

Lucy turned her back on him, opening and closing the door without another word. As she leaned against the closed door, tears rimmed her eyes, and she sank to the floor, wondering how she would ever get through the next morning's ordeal.

Finally, she stood, wiped her eyes, and was heading upstairs when the back door slammed.

Her son Rob appeared. "Hey, Mom, was that Dad's car I just saw?"

"Yup." She smiled at her oldest, a slimmer, younger version of his handsome father.

"What'd he want?"

"Nothing," she said, running her fingers through her hair.

"He's upset you."

"Just have to get through tomorrow."

"I can skip school and come."

"No, you can't. It's just paperwork. Chris says it'll take fifteen minutes."

"Dad still wants you back, you know."

"No, he doesn't."

"Does too. I heard him telling Uncle Mike that he was going to win you back."

Like that's gonna happen. She smiled at him. "Well, I think he's a little late."

"You could still call it off."

"No, sweetheart, I can't. We're done, your dad and me. Just like Grandma and Grandpa. No going back."

"Except Dad isn't Grandpa."

"No, but he's with another woman now. The woman he's been with for three years. We're over, sweetie."

"So are you with Mr. Morgan now?"

"We're seeing each other, yes."

"Do you love him?"

"I honestly don't know. He's a nice man. I enjoy his company."

"If it weren't for him, would you give Dad another chance?"

Is this what this is about? The spontaneous, concerned visit, bragging to his brother? she thought. *Rob's heard I'm dating, and he doesn't like it!*

"Richard has nothing to do with this, honey. Dad and I were broken up when I met him."

Rob paced beside the kitchen counter where they now stood. "Amy thinks so. I mean, she thinks you'd go back to Dad if it weren't for Mr. Morgan."

"Well, she's wrong, honey. I'm sorry." She reached forward and gave him a hug. His body was stiff and unyielding, but he didn't pull away. "What are your plans for the afternoon?"

"Soccer, then studying."

"Want something to eat?"

"No, thanks. I ate at the McNallys'," he said, referring to the family of his best friend, Andy. "I'm just gonna change and head back out."

Lucy sighed as he disappeared up the stairs. Someone was always leaving, or at least that was how it seemed.

CHAPTER 12

Lucy arrived at the County District Courthouse at eight thirty. No sign of Chris. Rob sat on a bench in the second-floor hallway, hunched over, elbows on his knees. When he spied her, he stood, ran his fingers through his hair, and adjusted his tie. Reflexive, familiar gestures.

"Morning," he said, giving her a grim half smile. He hadn't bothered to have his family's cutthroat attorney present for what the pompous Dick Garrison called "a trifling." He'd already done all the heavy lifting. Let Chris D'Angelo mop up.

She nodded but said nothing, taking a seat on the bench.

"You paying Chris for his time today?"

Lucy shrugged.

"Well, if he charges you, let me know, and I'll pay half."

Just as she bit back what would have been a sarcastic *don't bother*, Chris came up the stairs. "Morning, folks." He nodded at Rob, then sat beside her, patting Lucy's hand. "You ready?"

Lucy nodded, afraid to speak lest she break down.

"Okay, then, let's head in." Chris stood, extending his hand, which she took only until they reached the courtroom door. Rob opened it, and she passed by, the familiar scent of his lime aftershave somehow comforting.

There were a number of people waiting for their cases to be called. Lucy sat among the crowd of strangers and wished she were a million miles away. She decided to focus on Richard's kiss and block out the rest. Finally, their case was called, and Chris escorted her to the witness box. He asked her a series of questions to ascertain whether she did, indeed, wish to divorce Robert Whitcomb Brennan. She answered each one, her voice soft, tears streaming down her cheeks. *How strange to be saying such intimate things and crying openly with so many eyes watching.*

Then her time was over, and it was Rob's turn. As he spoke, she stared at the floor, his every word like a rebuke.

Later, as they walked out of the building, she grasped Chris's arm. She felt numb and impossibly cold. He had several documents for her to sign including one that changed her legal name back to Lucy Winthrop. They hugged at the car, then she slipped in and drove away without a look or word to her now officially ex-husband.

She had planned to go from court to the office, but now realized she needed time, so she drove home. The kids were at school and the house was quiet. As she wandered through the rooms, she decided that it was, indeed, time to move. She would talk to the kids. If they didn't object, she would start to look. Rob would probably keep the house, so it wasn't likely they would lose their childhood home. *Yes, time to move on. Family conference tonight,* she thought just as the doorbell rang.

"Richard?" she asked, puzzled as she opened the door to find him on her doorstep. "What are you doing here?"

"Thought I'd stop by to see if you're okay. It was court this morning, right?"

"Yes, but how did you know?"

"It's a small town. I heard talk in the Café yesterday."

"Of course you did." She gave him a wan smile.

"Would you rather be alone?" he asked, still standing outside in the cold.

"Oh, sorry... No. Do you want to come in? I'm afraid I won't be very good company."

"Not what I'm here for," he said, stepping in and folding her into his arms.

Just what I need, she thought, reveling in his warm embrace. *What I've needed all year and all morning.*

They stood in the hall for a long time before she said, "Want something? Coffee or tea?"

"Not particularly, but if you do, I'll join you."

They walked arm in arm into the family room and sat side by side, his strong arm circling her shoulders. Lucy rested her head on his chest and closed her eyes. "Thank you," she said softly as he took her hand.

"WHAT ARE YOU DOING HERE?" LOLLY ASKED AS LUCY STEPPED INTO the office shortly after noon.

"We have a ton of work to do. I thought I'd see if you guys wanted sandwiches. Where's Wolfie?"

"Post office. He'll be back soon. So, how was it? I thought you'd take the day off."

"Horrible, but Richard came by when I got home. That helped. And we have way too much to do for me to take the day off."

"So that was nice of him."

"Yeah, he just came, and we sat holding hands on the sofa. Then after a while, he left. It was nice of him."

"You sure you're okay?"

"Yes, thank you, mother hen. Ah, here's Wolfie." She took their lunch orders, then headed back out. The day had warmed, and the sun felt good on her cheeks as she walked the short distance to the Crab Café. Mercifully, the line was short. She was on her way out when Sandy Rodriguez pushed open the door.

"Hey, Lucy, how are you?"

"Fine."

"It was good of you to come out Saturday night." In another time period, Lolly's ex could have passed for a swashbuckler, with his broad shoulders and thick, dark hair curled round his shoulders. Coal-black eyes appraised every inch of her. They'd warned Lolly to stay away from him in high school, but who could resist once those bedroom eyes had you in their sights?

"Always want to support Marla."

"Sorry I didn't get over to talk to you guys. Band's not half-bad. We'll have 'em again." Sandy was always a bit full of himself. Warm, funny, and passionate, he was also used to getting his own way. People were drawn to him like a magnet, and he used that knowledge to his advantage.

"That's kind of you."

"Looks like there's a new man in your life."

"Excuse me?"

"Dick Morgan? Couldn't keep his hands off you?"

"We're friends," she said, thinking she had no interest in having this conversation with Sandy Rodriguez or anyone else, especially today!

"I know the family, you know. We go way back."

"Yes, Richard told me you worked for them one summer."

"Great times. Why we—"

"Sorry Sandy, will you excuse me? I've got lunch for the crew."

"I hear my buddy Wolfie's working for you?"

"Yup, gotta run. See you, Sandy."

As the Café door swung shut, Lucy let her breath out in a whoosh. *What a day, and it's only half over!*

"Dad, this is ridiculous," Gail Morgan said, hands on hips as she regarded the dining room table that now extended across the front hall and halfway into the living room. "Just have two or three tables. The kids can certainly be separate. Ava and Dan will bring Marta, I'm sure."

"Marta!" Richard said, slapping his forehead. "That's how we got to twenty!"

"Focus, Dad! The table?"

"Is perfect. We're all sitting together, and that's that."

Weezie came in from the kitchen, a sandwich wrap in her hand. "Even if we'll need a megaphone to communicate from one end to the other?"

He hugged her. "No one has to communicate from one end to the other. You chat with your tablemates. Think *Downton Abbey*."

Gail rolled her eyes. "Uh-huh. Well, then I'm seating myself next to someone interesting."

"That's the spirit," he said, clapping his hands.

"When are Pam, Ben, and Teddy getting in?" Weezie asked, referring to three of their siblings. Ava and Dan Fielding lived in town. Ben was in med school in Philadelphia, Teddy, the artist, in Providence and Pam, a social worker still resided in Maine, near where they had lived for many years.

"Just talked to her and Pam'll be here tomorrow," Gail said. "Ben not until Wednesday night, and Teddy'll just come for the day Thursday."

"Is Rich bringing Sara?" Weezie asked.

"Yup," her father said. "Hence the twenty."

Gail shook her head. "I hope your lady friend and her family know what they're getting into. It's gonna be a zoo."

Richard grinned, eyes running the length of the enormous makeshift table as he hugged his prickly daughter again. "A happy, loving zoo," he said.

CHAPTER 13

"Welcome, welcome!" Richard stepped aside as Lucy and her mother, Harriet, Kyle and their youngest sister Hazel behind them, stepped into the wide front hall. There was a dining room table in front of them, jutting out from the next room.

"Pay no attention to that table. We're in here. Let me take your coats. Oh, this is Callie." He thrust the pile of coats into the arms of a slender blonde.

"Hi," she said, heading up the stairs with her pile.

"Callie's our cook, housekeeper, and everything else around here. Come."

He took Helen's arm and led the group into the family room at the rear of the house. Although cavernous, the room felt warm and inviting, with fires blazing in stone fireplaces at either end. The room had several seating areas with sectionals and chairs, and one corner area was furnished with smaller chairs, bookshelves, and bins of toys. A small boy and girl sat on the floor playing with a plump young woman with dirty blonde hair pulled back in a ponytail.

"Those are two of my three grandchildren, Sasha and Cameron, and their wonderful nanny, Marta. Their parents are around here somewhere. I can't remember, do you know Dan and Ava?" He addressed his question to Harriet.

She nodded. "Yes, Dan's always great when we take field trips to the Lab, and Ava's taught several programs for us."

In a blur of introductions, Richard brought them to say hello to each family member. Helen began a conversation with Teddy about leaded glass work, while Kyle and Harriet chatted with Rich and Ben about horses, the mustang program, and future plans. After Richard handed her a glass of white wine, he hurried off to the kitchen, and Lucy was left standing with Gail and Pamela Morgan.

"Your dad says you're thinking of relocating down this way," she said to Pamela.

The petite strawberry blonde shrugged, then smiled at her. "Dad's dream, but I'm tempted. It's beautiful around here, and I'm getting tired of Maine winters."

"Do you ski?"

"Some, but mostly snowshoeing."

"I love snowshoeing," Lucy said, "but haven't done much of it the past few years."

"So you've always lived here?" Gail said. She looked rather bored with the whole conversation.

"Since high school, when my mom moved here permanently, but we summered here most of our childhood."

"So your mom's here too?" Pam said.

"Yes, her cottage is just outside the village, toward the Point."

"Is that where you summered?" Gail asked.

"Yes."

"Where did you live before?"

"New Bedford. My dad's family home was there."

"And I understand your former husband has a medical practice here?" Gail said.

Former husband of three days. Lucy felt as if she were getting the third degree. "Yes."

"So you met here?" Pam asked.

"Yes, he grew up here, or in Somers."

"In that lovely house where you now reside?" Gail asked.

"Yes, but maybe not for long," Lucy replied. A change of subject was definitely in order! "So how do *you* like living here?" she asked, directing her attention to Gail.

"Would you excuse me?" Gail said. "It looks like Callie needs help."

Pam watched her sister's hasty retreat, then turned back to Lucy. "She doesn't know how to answer that question. Gail's never been able to leave home but doesn't want to admit it."

"What about college?"

"Commuted to University of Maine for her undergrad and masters. Never left home, never left our parents. Mom's death was difficult on all of us, but Gail took it especially hard."

"Your mother sounds like a remarkable woman."

Pam gave her a crooked smile. "She was by all accounts. I don't really remember her. I was only three when she died."

At that moment, Hazel joined them. "This is some house and some property," she said, smiling from one to the other. Dark-haired with gray-blue eyes that sparkled with light, Hazel was the child of Helen's second husband, Tim. Petite and athletic, she was an avid hiker.

"Dad's never been known to do things halfway," Pam said.

"Like his brother," Lucy said. "Have you ever been to Saguaro Valley?"

"No, but we're going after Weezie's description," Ben Morgan said, coming up behind them, arm circling his sister's shoulders. "I was named for my uncle, and I hear there are a lot of Bens running around out there."

Lucy laughed. "Yes, too many! One never knows who'll come if you call 'Ben' in that crowd."

"Hey, guys," Richard said. "Glad you're getting acquainted."

He put his arm around Lucy, and she was relieved Gail had departed. Pam and Ben didn't seem to mind. Hazel's radar was up, and she winked at her.

"Turkey's been carved, sideboards are groaning with food, and it's time to find your seats," the family patriarch said. "Shall we?"

Plates laden with food, Richard led Lucy to her seat to his right,

Helen beside her, then Hazel. Gail was seated across from Lucy on her father's left. Lucy watched Gail take the seat that was clearly hers and wondered if she would ever accept another woman in her father's life. She peered down the table and smiled at Harriet. She and Kyle were surrounded by his cousins—Ava, Dan, and their children, Teddy, Ben, and the farm's assistant foreman, Dennis Farrell. Clearly in his element, Kyle was laughing and joking with the children.

"What a wonderful father he'll make," Helen said, following her gaze.

"Yes." Lucy recalled how many times people had remarked about what a great dad Rob was and how lucky she was.

"Penny for your thoughts." Richard reached over to squeeze her hand.

Startled, she smiled at him. "I was wondering how I'll ever finish all this delicious food."

"You're not a very good liar, Lucy Winthrop."

"Sorry."

"No apologies necessary. If I can help, let me know, and please don't feel you have to eat it all. Callie always makes enough for an army."

"All our mom's favorite recipes," Gail said. "It's a tradition. Callie makes them every Thanksgiving."

"Well, everything is wonderful," Helen said. "Your mother must have been an excellent cook."

"Oh, she was," Gail said. "All types of food too, since we lived all over the world."

"And had excellent chefs in most of our homes," her father said, winking at Helen.

"I'm afraid I'm not much of a cook," Helen said. "When Lucy was little, the Winthrops' cook, Kitty, prepared all the meals. She was an especially good baker. I still dream of her pies, cookies, and breads."

"You eat well out west too," Richard said. "Those two ladies, Carmela and that raven-haired beauty of Spark's, are something."

Helen chuckled. "Aria."

"Yes, the lovely Aria. What a cook."

"I believe she prefers to be called a chef," Lucy said, smiling at her mother. She had thoroughly enjoyed her stay at Spark Foster's, the gourmet meals and the constant pampering along with the family's contagious warmth.

"Gotta get that crew out this way," Richard said. "Maybe when we officially open the farm, we could get Foster to fly 'em all out in his private jet."

Dinner conversation continued to be lively, wine flowing throughout. Finally, Callie set out twelve pies on the sideboards along with bowls of ice cream and whipped cream. Silver urns with coffee and hot water sat at either end with colorful cups and mugs. "This is amazing," Hazel whispered as the sisters stood, trying to decide which pies to try.

Harriet nodded. "I think this spread gives the Morgans and Spark a run for their money, at least on the dessert end."

"I've gotta get out there," Hazel said, selecting a sliver of creamy chocolate lace pie.

"Yes, you do," Harriet said. "And you will as soon as we decide on the big day."

"That's gonna be quite something," Lucy said, eyeing a pie with meringue topping almost a foot high.

"And Kyle says he's inviting all this crew," Harriet whispered. "Wild doesn't even begin to describe it!"

"Where will they put us all?"

Lucy laughed. "You wait. They have enough beds for an army." She leaned against Hazel's shoulder. After the rawness of the past week, it felt so good to be laughing with her sister. Comforting.

"I don't know when I've seen a prettier pair of sisters," Richard said, "My girls too, of course."

"This has been lovely, Richard," she said, leaning against him as his arm circled her shoulders. "Thank you for including us."

"The first of many, my dear Lucy. The first of many."

~

THE HOUSE WAS QUIET AND EMPTY WHEN SHE GOT HOME. AS SHE closed the door behind her, Lucy smiled, thinking of Richard and his sweeping her into the front hall closet for a surreptitious kiss as they prepared to leave. "I'd keep you here all night if I could get away with it," he'd whispered, kissing her deeply, strong hands caressing her.

Sadness lingered, but Richard Morgan's arms and the company of her family had taken the edge off the holiday and made it bearable. Holidays were always the hardest.

CHAPTER 14

L olly pouted behind a wall of boxes. They were discussing Christmas, and Lolly was moaning about having to spend it with "my dysfunctional family."

"So come to my house," Lucy said. "Kyle and Harriet are in Saguaro, but it'll still be a fun group—the kids, Mum, and Frankie. Clara and Will were planning to come, but she and the kids have the flu. Hazel offered to go down to help Will, so she won't be here either. We'd love to have you and Maisie."

"Maisie's with her dad."

"All the more reason for you to come to my house. Spend the night if you want."

"Mom'd be crushed."

"Bring her. Mum would be thrilled to have another Darn Yarner. Frankie's staying over. It'll be a pajama party."

"I'll ask, but then there's Marla."

"Who's also welcome."

"She might go to the city to be with Dad. I'll check with Mom and let you know. Fun as it sounds, we'll probably skip the sleepover. I like my own bed."

Lolly turned to their assistant, who was conspicuously quiet behind the boxes. "What's your crew doing, Wolfie?"

"We'll be at Dan and Ava's. Dad wanted to do it at the farmhouse, but Ava insisted. We'll have Christmas Eve dinner at Dad's. Pam's not coming. She's going to my aunt's. She lives outside of Augusta."

I am so sick of holiday orchestrations! Lucy thought. *Let's just skip to New Year's and be done with it.* What a difference from years past when Christmases had been joyful and full of familiar rituals and traditions. Then there were their childhood Christmases at Hill House with her grandparents. Moments of fun, delicious food, and picture-postcard decorations along with the unpredictable day-to-day life with an alcoholic father. His drinking escalated during most holidays.

Once her mother moved them to Horseshoe Crab Cove, Christmases had been peaceful and full of quiet joy. Helen made sure of that. Tiny treats left by their doors each morning of Advent, the smell of gingerbread and the excitement of creating handmade gifts. The two years of her mother and Tim's marriage before his untimely death were the happiest Christmases Lucy could remember. And, of course, her own family celebrations and all the cherished traditions she and Rob had built together. Their loss had been shattering. She shook herself. *No sense dwelling on what I cannot change.*

"Well, you, Lolly, and you, Wolfie, are both welcome to come, or stop by on Christmas or Christmas Eve. Bring whomever you like. Now shall we get to work?"

They'd been working for several hours when Lucy's cell rang. She smiled, spying Richard's name. "Hello?"

"Hi. How are you?"

"Buried in mailers and boxes. I don't know what we did before your son. Our holiday orders have all come in at once. How are you?"

"Great. I'm actually on Main Street, strolling your way, and I wondered if I could take you or even your whole crew to lunch at the Café?"

"Hold on, I'll ask. Guys, this is Richard. He wants to take us to lunch."

"No can do," Lolly said. "I've got to meet Mom at the house. Some sort of crisis."

"Wolfie?" Lucy asked, peering over the wall of boxes.

"Thanks, but I'm good. I brought lunch."

"Richard? You still there?"

"Yup."

"Just me?"

"Perfect. Don't tell the others, but I was hoping things might turn out that way."

"Meet you in ten?"

"Will do. I'll get us a table."

"Okay if I knock off and eat out on the balcony?" Wolfie asked. "The mention of lunch made me hungry."

"Of course," Lucy said, eyeing him, then her partner. As he closed the door behind him, she looked over at Lolly. "Does your mom really have a crisis?"

"No, but no one likes to be a third wheel."

"Don't be ridiculous."

"I am going over to the house. She wants my help with something. Might as well go at lunchtime. There'll be lots of great food 'cause they're prepping for this weekend's wedding, testing a bunch of new recipes."

Mavis LaSalle was reputed to have one of the finest chefs on the eastern seaboard. The Cove, her wedding and event venue, employed a full-time catering staff, with Kendall Reese at the helm. Kendall's cuisine had been featured in numerous magazines, and she was constantly getting offers to have her own cooking show. So far, she was content at the Cove, but Mavis fretted constantly about how long they'd be able to keep her.

"So, I guess I'll head out," Lucy said, grabbing her purse. "See you in about an hour."

"You betcha."

❦

ALWAYS THE GENTLEMAN, RICHARD STOOD AS SHE APPROACHED THE table. She was about to say hello when a voice called from her side.

"Hey, Lucy." It was Chuck Beaman, Rob's partner and best friend. They had gone through medical school together and started the practice in the Cove right after.

"Hi, Chuck," she said as the stocky physician hopped up and grabbed her in a bear hug. Chuck had a baby face, untouched by the years, freckles, blue eyes and a ruddy complexion. Unlike his friend and business partner, Chuck was not a runner. More of a weekend warrior, he always said, whether it was a pickup rugby game or a game of tennis.

"How are you?"

"Great, thanks. I'm actually meeting someone," she said gesturing toward Richard, who was observing with bemused attention.

"Ah, my newest patient," Chuck said, waving over her shoulder. "Nice guy. Well, I'll let you go. You look great, by the way." His pale eyes ran over her, appraising every inch. Single, Chuck was always on the prowl.

"Thanks," she said. "Take care." As she moved by him, Chuck's hand grazed her hip and lingered a bit longer than appropriate. *Geez!*

"Small town," Richard said, pecking her cheek as he waited for her to sit.

"Yup."

"I like small towns, but they can get a little too small at times."

"Yes, they can."

"Do I need to find a doc in Somers or farther afield?"

She laughed. "No, Chuck may be a bit of a lecher, but he's discreet."

"Lecher? Not sure I like the sound of that. How are you? You look lovely." And she did, her cheeks rosy, her hair windblown and free. She was in jeans and a pale blue sweater, a becoming scarf in swirling blues and greens tied round her neck.

"Thank you. You too." He wore a marled cotton sweater, the charcoal gray picking up the light in his dark eyes. Lucy sighed. *Is it fair to this kind, handsome man to lead him on when I'm such a wreck?*

They both ordered soup and shared a grilled bacon and cheese sandwich, one of the Café's specialties. As she sipped iced tea, her phone buzzed, and she saw RB, indicating her ex-Rob's name. She frowned, slipping the phone into her purse.

"If you need to get that, it's fine," he said.

"No, it's not fine. I'm with you!" she said, more vehemently than she intended. "It's Rob, my ex, not my son. Now that the papers are final, he's decided he wants to give us another chance."

"Oh?"

"I'm sorry," she said, blushing. "I didn't mean to blurt that out. You don't need to hear about my problems."

He reached across the table and took her hand. "I'm happy to hear your problems and anything else. Has this been going on for a while?"

"Since he saw us together at Sandy's. He doesn't want me back, he just doesn't want me with anyone else. He's very competitive, and I suspect his relationship with Chloe may not be turning out as he hoped."

"Must be confusing for you." His fingers gently massaged her palm, and Lucy gazed up to find eyes full of concern.

"Not in the least. We are over, finished, done."

"Are you sure?"

"Yes...no...oh, Richard, I'm so sorry! This is just what you need." She gulped, taking a slow, deep breath. "I absolutely do not want to get back together with Rob. It's just that sometimes life seems to be spinning out of control. There's nothing familiar. Everything's changing."

He smiled. "That's life. Everything's always been changing. It's just sometimes we notice, sometimes we don't."

She smiled at him. "How did you get so wise?"

He chuckled, leaning back in his chair. "Me, wise? Hardly. Just old. I've been knocking around for over twenty years tryin' to figure things out."

"And?" Lucy asked.

"And you're the first person I've ever wanted to try and figure things out with."

She gave him a rueful smile. "Too bad I'm such a basket case."

"You'll get there."

"Maybe. I've made an appointment to see my sister's therapist next week."

"A positive step."

"Maybe," she said. "Now let's talk about something else. Have Gus and his family arrived?"

"Tomorrow. I'd love it if you'd come to dinner Friday. Small dinner to welcome them before they head to Connecticut to spend Christmas with Lynn's family."

"I'd love to come. What can I bring?"

"Your beautiful self."

She smiled. "I'll bring wine."

"You know, I'd love to find a quiet spot and kiss your socks off," he said, grinning.

Lucy laughed. "Now that's an expression I haven't heard in a while."

CHAPTER 15

Lucy had been back in the office no more than fifteen minutes when Rob Brennan appeared.

Lolly spied him first. "What do you want?"

"Lucy around?"

She stepped from behind a bookshelf. "Rob, what are you doing here?"

Instead of answering, her ex-husband extended hand to Wolfie. "Rob Brennan."

"Hey, man," Wolfie said, shaking his hand but not identifying himself.

"Sorry, this is Wolfie," Lucy said.

"High time you hired help."

Trying to keep irritation from her voice, she said, "What is it, Rob? As you can see, we're really busy."

"Can I talk to you for a sec?" He gestured toward the door.

Lucy followed him into the hall, taking several deep breaths as she closed the door behind them. "So?"

"Chuck said he ran into you."

"Yes."

"Said you looked like a million bucks, and you do."

"So you left your patients and the office to come over and tell me that?"

"No... Yes... Not exactly. I just wanted to see you."

"Why?"

"I miss you. You are my best friend."

Were, she thought, *until you trampled all over that friendship screwing Chloe Birdsong. What kind of a name is that anyway?* "Well, I'm not sure I can help you with that."

"I can't talk to Chloe like I talk to you."

Maybe that's because she's a gazillion years younger? "Rob, I'm sorry to hear that, but I still have no idea what you think I can do about it."

"I think I made a huge mistake."

Lucy stared at him, incredulous. Was this jealousy speaking? His competitive streak coming out? "I'm sorry about that, but it's too late."

"Don't say that!" he said, reaching out, trying to take her hands.

Lucy stepped back out of reach. "I'm not sure where this is coming from, but I can't do this with you. Six months ago, I would have leapt into your arms, but it's over. We're over."

"It's Morgan, isn't it? Do you love him?"

"That's none of your business, and this conversation is over."

"The kids think you do."

Lucy raised her hands. "Stop! Enough! And you damn well better not put the kids in the middle of this."

"Sorry, I'm not. That was a stupid remark."

"Yes, it was."

"I was thinking of taking your mom to lunch. What do you think?"

Shocked, she shook her head. "I have no idea. Mom's her own person."

"Probably hates me, huh? Like your sisters."

"No one hates you. You were like a son and brother to them."

"Not anymore."

Suddenly weary and sad, she said, "Go back to the office, Rob. Or go home. Chloe is your soft place now, your best friend and your confidante. You need to work on things with her, not me."

"I'm sorry, Luce."

Hand on the doorknob, inwardly seething at his use of his pet name for her, she said, "Me too. Now I've got to get back."

"Sorry for disturbing you. It won't happen again."

Yeah, right, she thought closing the door behind her. *And pigs'll be flying through the village at dusk.*

Lolly looked up, and before she could speak, Lucy raised her hand. "Don't want to talk about it."

"She already knows the Caseys. We don't," Gail Morgan said, frowning as they sat in the farmhouse dining room discussing Friday's welcome dinner for Lynn Manguilli, Gus Casey, and his kids.

Her brother Rich leaned back in his chair. "By that reasoning, we shouldn't invite Weezie and Wolfie. They know those guys too."

"Ha-ha," Gail said, glaring at him.

"Then it's settled. Lucy, Kyle, and Harriet and us," Richard said. "Callie's getting steamers and lobsters 'cause Lynn loves them."

"But she's pregnant," Weezie said. "Can she eat that stuff?"

"According to Gus, yes," her father said. "Now let's move on. Where are we with the mustangs?"

"They arrive in a week or two. We'll have the exact date soon," Rich said.

"And is all the equipment Gus ordered in?"

"Most of it."

"Okay, then. I understand from Dennis that we've had a couple of inquiries about boarding horses," Richard said.

Rich nodded. "Yup, but Gus doesn't think we should commit to anything until the mustangs are settled and he's here."

"Good plan. Weezie, what's your thinking about that?"

"Oh, so now you're asking me?"

"I always value your input, sweetie."

"I think we should take boarders, and I'd also like to start a 4 H program in the spring. There's real interest in that, apparently."

Richard smiled at his dark-haired daughter. "Go for it. Rich, liability there?"

"I'll check."

"Okay, then. We set?"

As the others disappeared, Richard turned to his son. "Where are we with the vintner?"

"Still negotiating. He wants living quarters."

"We can do that. Either build something or rent something in town."

"He wants to bring his assistant."

"Think we can handle it?"

"Not only do I think we can handle it, I think it's essential. She sounds like she's his apprentice, and Mr. Ravensbrook isn't getting any younger."

"You think we're overextending, son?"

Rich smiled at his father. "Maybe, but you...we can afford it."

"Good man."

Rich gathered his papers, preparing to return to his office on the second floor of the main barn.

"Got one more minute?" Richard said.

His son stopped what he was doing. "Sure, what's up?"

"Are you okay about my dating Lucy?"

"Of course."

"I know Gail's not keen on her."

"It's not Lucy," Rich said. "It's that she senses this relationship is different."

"It is. I've fallen hard."

"She's a great person. I'm happy for you, Dad."

"Did any of the others have an opinion?"

"Honestly, we didn't discuss it except to say we were glad you seemed happy. And Wolfie clearly likes her. Guy ran away from home to live at her house."

Richard laughed. "Well, there is that."

"Don't worry about Gail. She'll come around."

"I wish she'd spread her wings a bit, find someone to date," Richard said. "It isn't healthy for her to be closeted away here."

"She's a homebody. Always has been."

"Well, I'm gonna make it my business to find her a nice fellow."

Rich grimaced. "I'd leave that alone if I were you."

"We'll see. How's your girl anyway? Haven't seen her lately."

"We're kind of taking a break," he said, referring to Sara Gregson, a yoga instructor in the village whom he'd been seeing for a few months. "We've decided to be friends so I can still take her classes.

"Lucy's big on yoga. Maybe I should give it a try."

Rich smiled at his father. "Good idea. Sara's a great teacher, and she's got lots of beginner DVDs."

As Rich headed out, his father reached for his phone, wanting to hear Lucy's voice. Then he paused and decided, *Don't make a pest of yourself, you old coot.*

CHAPTER 16

"Gail's in fine form tonight," Harriet whispered to her sister as the two sat at the kitchen island. Nearby, tossing a huge bowl of salad, Callie, Richard's cook, grinned.

Lucy poked her sister. "Shush! Sorry, Callie. Pay no attention to her."

The lady in question was in the adjacent family room draped on her father's arm playing hostess as she and her father made introductions and got drinks for everyone. From time to time, Gail glanced in their direction, a smug smile on her face.

"Don't take it personally. She's just scared," Callie said as she passed them, bowl in hand.

Surprised, Lucy stared at Callie, then Harriet. At that moment, Lynn Manguilli approached to say hello, Dulcie Casey beside her, holding her hand. "Hi, Winthrop sisters. So good to see you both."

They each hugged her. Six months pregnant, Lynn looked lovely in a flowing peasant blouse, jeans, and sneakers. Her long dark hair was loose, falling down her back in thick waves.

"We're so glad to see you! You look great!" Harriet said. "And Dulcie too." She knelt down so she was eye height with the shy child and was rewarded by a sweet smile.

"You've gotten so big since I saw you last June," Lucy said to Dulcie before turning to Lynn. "Are you all settled in?"

"Most of our things are in storage," Lynn said. "Didn't seem worth it to move them into the rental 'cause it's furnished."

"How long before your house is finished?" Harriet asked as Kyle came up beside her, winking at Dulcie.

"Uncle Dick's got 'em working overtime to get it ready."

"I hope not during the holidays," Lynn said. "We're fine in the rental. It's real cute. Right on the water with a dock. Be fun to be there in the summer."

"We were so sorry to hear about your mom," Harriet said.

"Thanks. Yes, it's been a shock for everyone, especially her. I don't know if anyone's told you, but it's pancreatic cancer. The prognosis is grim, but we're all going to try and be there for her, and she's determined to fight it."

"I'm sure it's a great comfort to have you closer. And your siblings are nearby too, right?" Lucy said.

"Yes, Barry lives in New Haven, and Barb's at UConn. Against Mother's wishes, she's proposing to take a leave of absence from school."

"If there's anything we can do to help, please let us know," Lucy said. "My daughter Amy loves to babysit, as does Rob, my son."

"And there are plenty of Hampton Meeting students who love to sit too," Harriet said.

"Thank you. Both the kids are going to start at Red Brick after the new year. We thought about keeping them home since I don't have a job, but they do love school, and it's only a half day. Plus, if I have to go to Connecticut for the day, they have after care while Gus is working. He claims he can take them to the farm anytime, but I'm not sure that's true."

"Oh, yes it is!" Weezie said, coming from behind, hugging Lynn. "We would love to have them anytime."

"And here are some of the prettiest girls on the planet," Richard said, gently moving out of Gail's reach, his arms round Lucy's and Weezie's shoulders.

With a scowl, Gail walked away as Gus joined them, his son Cal in his arms. "Hi, ladies," he said. "Great to see you for my second meal of lobsters and clams ever."

"These guys are the best, according to my sources in town," Richard said.

"Your sources are correct," Lucy said. "Salters puts on the best winter boils and summer bakes in the area."

"This is a big change for you all, isn't it?" Weezie said. "I mean, Saguaro was a really cool place. Is this permanent, do you think?"

Lucy stared at Richard's daughter, surprised at what seemed like insensitive questions.

Lynn paused long enough for Gus to step in. "Lynn gave up a lot to come east. Dear friends and that wonderful school she and Polly built. The impetus was clearly her mom's illness and wanting to be closer, but this is a great opportunity for me. If we hadn't found a really good replacement for me at Valley Stables, I'd still be there, but we did."

"And we are the lucky ones," Richard said. "Lucy, can I steal you for a minute?" He took her hand and led her out of the kitchen toward the front of the house to his office, off the front hallway. He closed the French doors behind them and drew her close, against the wall, hidden from passersby.

"Is everything okay?" she said.

"Everything's perfect. I just wanted you to myself for a minute. I've missed you this week." Before she could respond, his lips captured hers in a deep, lingering kiss.

"Richard!" she whispered breathlessly, her body aching for him. "What if someone comes by?"

"They can't see us. You look beautiful tonight."

She almost said *you always say that*, but caught herself. She loved his sweet compliments. She wore jeans, a pale pink turtleneck, and blue cashmere sweater. Nothing fancy, but she felt comfortable and sexy as his hands caressed her back. "Thank you."

Gently pushing her turtleneck aside, he trailed kisses down her neck, his hands cupping her full, round breasts, fingers teasing her nipples to hardness. "This is not a good idea," she whispered huskily as he grew hard against her belly.

"Oh yes it is," he said, slipping his hand inside her jeans, fingers creeping downward until he touched her moist warmth. "And you want me as much as I do you."

"Not here, not now!"

"Okay, well, if you're chicken, we'd better go back."

In answer, she unzipped her jeans and dropped them and her panties to the floor. "Okay, if you insist. No one's calling me chicken, Richard Morgan. So...what are you gonna do about it?"

"Oh baby," he whispered, dropping his jeans, a condom already in hand. "Come to Papa." He slipped the condom on, then lifted her to straddle him. As Lucy leaned back, arching her back, he plunged into her. "This is where I want to be. That's right, baby, give me more, and more and more!"

Lucy splayed her arms out against the wall, lost in a riot of sensation as every thrust brought him deeper, the ebb and flow of their lovemaking almost excruciating. "Oh, Richard, oh, oh, oh!" Her voice came out in a whisper yet felt like a scream in her head. She realized they were far from silent as their bodies knocked and bumped against the wall, but she didn't care. *Let the whole world find us, as long as he never stops!* were her last coherent thoughts as they brought each other to a crackling, white-hot climax.

In the aftermath, Richard leaned against her, wrapping her arms around his shoulders. "Are you okay?" he whispered.

She nodded, unable to speak. Suddenly, they heard voices in the hall and Rich calling, "Dad!"

"Shit!" Richard said, stifling a laugh. They hid in the darkness of the office, dressing quickly. When the voices receded, he went to the door, then turned back, taking her hand. "Come on, the coast is clear." He led her out the front door into the cold evening air.

"What are you doing?"

"Giving you a tour of the outside. We can go in through the kitchen door."

"Like we've been strolling around with no coats in the freezing cold?" Lucy asked, gazing over at him in the light of the front walk. "Do I look okay?"

"You look like you've been well fucked, my girl."

Surprised at his language, she said, "Richard this isn't funny! Do I look disheveled?"

"No, you look great. Your hair may be a little mussed, but there's a bit of a breeze tonight."

"This is craziness!" she said. "Let's get inside quickly! Maybe I can duck into the bathroom. It's freezing!"

When they reached the kitchen door, he went in first, hiding her as she slipped into the bathroom off the mudroom. As she smoothed her hair and splashed water on her face, she heard voices asking him, "Where have you been? The food's all ready."

When Lucy emerged, there was no one about, and she headed through the back pantry into the kitchen. Callie was filling baskets with fresh bread. She looked up and smiled. "He's in the dining room. Said to tell you he's saving you a seat."

"Thanks," Lucy said, face bright red now.

As she made her way into the dining room, Harriet caught her. "What in the world have you been up to, sister of mine?"

"Never mind! It's not what it looks like."

"Oh, honey, everyone in this room knows what it looks like, sound effects and all."

Stricken, Lucy stared at her. "Really? Everyone?"

"Well, the kids may have missed it."

"I've got to get out of here now!"

"Oh no you don't," Richard said, appearing at her side. "If I'm staying, you are too."

Lucy dared not look at Gail or the others and barely tasted the excellent chowder. Another glass of wine helped calm her, but, mortified, she was counting the minutes until she could escape.

As the dinner conversation became lively, she finally relaxed. Occasionally, Richard would reach over and squeeze her hand, sometimes with a wink. As Callie served dessert, homemade ice cream sandwiches, he leaned over and said, "I can't remember when clams and lobster tasted so good. We'll have to do this again."

Lucy flushed crimson as she suppressed a giggle. *Crazy, crazy, crazy! I will never live this down!*

CHAPTER 17

Three days before Christmas, Lucy left work early to do some shopping. When she arrived at home, the house was quiet, both kids at their father's for dinner. She set the bags on the kitchen island and began assembling wrapping paper, scissors, ribbons, and tape. With any luck, she would complete all her wrapping and be ready for Christmas. She had just put a pot of soup on the stove when the doorbell rang.

She opened it, surprised to find Gail Morgan. "Gail. Hi."

"May I come in?"

"Of course. Can I get you something? Tea? Glass of wine? Seltzer? Beer?"

"I'm fine, thanks. I won't stay long."

"Throw your jacket anywhere," she said as she ushered her into the family room. Lucy sat on one end of the sofa and said, "Please, sit."

Coat still on, Gail took a chair opposite, sitting with a stiff back. "I'm sorry to barge in, but after the other night, I felt it was my duty to say something."

"Excuse me?"

"I hardly know where to begin. My siblings and I were horrified by your behavior. It's bad enough that you've thrown yourself at our father since you laid eyes on him in Arizona. Now, in the middle of a dinner party, you drag him off and subject us all to that!"

Lucy sat quietly, willing herself to take slow, deep breaths. Although she regretted the public nature of their lovemaking, she was neither ashamed nor sorry. She was also loath to defend or explain herself to Richard's angry daughter. Finally, she said, "I'm sorry you were horrified. It would not have been my choice to have things turn out that way. It was a mistake, of course. What should have been a private moment between your father and me was not."

Gail huffed, looking out the slider toward the winter gardens still bright with ornamental cabbages and bittersweet. "You're not the first, you know."

"I'm sorry? What?"

"You're just the latest in a long string of lovers. Dad grabs hold of someone for a short time, then moves on. Futile attempts to replace our mom, which he never will."

"I don't know about your father's other relationships, but no one will replace your mom. That's a given."

Gail paused, her face registering surprise before the scowl returned. "Then what do you think you're doing? A recent divorcee, looking for love and someone to pay the bills?"

That's enough. She willed her voice to stay calm. "What is it you want from me, Gail?"

"Break it off. Sure, Dad'll be upset at first, but he'll get over it. We have to live here. We're working hard to establish a business, and having him acting like Casanova, screwing women in dark corners, is not good for his reputation or business."

"This happened in his home, not on Main Street."

"My home!"

"Yes, of course, but it was in a private home, not on Main Street. It was also a one-time thing."

"What about Sandy's?"

"How did you—?"

Gail smirked. "Then it is true. I thought Weezie was exaggerating."

"Gail, this conversation has gone on long enough. It's insulting to me and your father."

"Does your mother know about your wildly inappropriate behavior?"

"That's none of your business."

"The village is *her* home too. I should think you'd want to respect her."

"My mother is the most nonjudgmental person I know."

"Too bad my dad didn't find her first. More his age."

"That's enough. Because you are Richard's daughter, I will pretend this never happened, but I think it's time for you to go."

"I'll go, but this happened and will continue to happen until you leave him alone."

"Does your father know you're here?"

"That's none of your business."

"I'll take that as a no."

Gail shrugged. "Tell him. What do I care?"

Lucy stood. "I hope someday you'll get help for all this anger and bitterness."

"Like I care what you think. Goodbye, Ms. Brennan." With those words, she stormed out, slamming the front door behind her.

Lucy sat down, her body trembling, rubbing her arms as a sudden chill came over her. *Thank goodness my appointment with Elise is tomorrow!*

WOLFIE SAT ALONE SORTING ORDERS WHEN LUCY GOT TO THE OFFICE the following morning. "Oh, Wolfie," she said. "What did we do without you?"

He grinned. "Almost ready to head down to the post office."

"Where's Lolly?"

"Said she had to run a couple of errands and would be back by eleven."

"Good. I have an appointment at twelve."

"You know they have shipping services that do all this, and they'd cost a lot less than you're paying me. Several of my dad's businesses use 'em."

"Are you unhappy here?"

"Not at all. Just trying to help. You guys have been great to me."

"Well, we like the human touch, so you can have a job as long as you want it. Things slow down after the holidays, but then we start doing all the book fairs."

"I'm in, although I promised my dad I'd at least learn about the vineyard business once his guy gets there."

"That's a great opportunity for you."

"Yeah, but it means getting sucked back into the family."

"And that's a problem?"

He shrugged. "Rich and Weezie are okay, but Gail and I don't get along."

Lucy gazed at Richard's handsome youngest son, "Adonis," as Lolly called him, and wondered again about the Morgan family dynamics. "Wolfie, I want to say something to you, and I hope I won't embarrass you."

He grinned. "If it's about the other night, don't torture yourself. I was cool with it, especially since it sent Gail right through the ceiling."

"Still, I'm sorry. We were very indiscreet, your dad and I."

"You know he's crazy about you."

"And I'm very fond of him too."

"No, I mean gaga, head over heels, crazy. That's why my sister's so bent out of shape."

"Rich and Weezie too?"

"Nah, they could care less. Neither do Ava, Ben, or Teddy. Haven't asked Pam, but I think it's great. I never knew my mom, but from what I've been told, Dad's been looking for someone since she died. Quite unsuccessfully, I might add. This has been just fine with Gail since she likes ruling the roost. Doesn't want anyone to replace our mother. You're different. She can see that, and she's scared shitless."

As she listened, Lucy realized that this was the longest

conversation she'd ever had with Wolfie, who was a taciturn soul of few words. "Then we go and do what we did the other night! Poor Gail." She could feel the red creeping up her neck flushing her cheeks.

He stood with his hands resting on the cart of boxes and mailers. "Like I said, don't sweat it. Things'll blow over. I'll just get these over and come back for the rest."

Lucy sat at her desk and buried her head in her hands. She could hear Lolly greeting Wolfie in the hall as he headed to the elevator. *Oh Lord, here we go!*

"What's up with you?" her partner asked. "You're red as a beet."

"We... I brought up the other night. To apologize."

"And?"

"You know Wolfie. He was fine with it."

"So why do you look like a shiny red tomato?"

"Because I'm obviously *not* fine with it."

"Did you tell him about Gail's visit?"

"No, and I won't."

"You going to tell Richard?"

"I honestly don't know. Maybe I'll explore this with Elise. You remember I have that appointment at noon?"

"Yup."

"We're backed up, aren't we?"

"Not too bad, although I don't know what we would have done without our amazing assistant."

"I just told him that."

"Right before you apologized for screwing his dad right under his nose?"

"Ha-ha. Can we please change the subject? I think if we work really hard, we can get everything mailed by noon tomorrow." They were taking a week off between Christmas and new year's. Lucy couldn't wait.

CHAPTER 18

Elise Nolan's office was above Village Books, where Lucy had run the children's room until the past year when Merlin's Closet had grown too big to do both. The office was two rooms with a bathroom down the hall. A small waiting room with a humming noise machine led to a cozy room with overstuffed chairs, a sofa, small refrigerator, and several side tables, one holding an electric teapot and a basket of assorted tea bags, packets of instant coffee, honey, and sugar.

A runner, Elise was petite and lean, dressed today in leggings and a soft green tunic. Her coal-black eyes sparkled, and her dark-brown cropped hair was damp, as if she'd recently showered.

"Come in, so good to see you," she said. "Just boiled water. Would you like tea or instant coffee? I also have water in the fridge."

"Tea would be great, thanks."

Elise offered her the basket of tea bags and a brightly colored ceramic mug. Lucy selected Earl Grey, and Elise followed suit, then invited her to sit. She sank into the large, incredibly comfortable overstuffed chair and took a tentative sip of tea, the scent of bergamot filling her senses.

"So how can I help?" Elise asked, her voice neutral, but inviting.

"Well, I've just gone through a nightmarish year that included a very abrupt and painful separation and recent divorce. Now I'm testing the dating waters and worry that I may have jumped into the deep end too soon. Would it be okay if I give you a quick summary?"

"Please, take as long as you need."

Lucy told her about Rob's infidelity and the sadness and pain of all that. She then described his recent behavior, which she suspected was a response to her budding relationship with Richard. Then she recounted her's and Richard's courtship, concluding with the dinner at the farmhouse and their not so private lovemaking.

Elise smiled and said, "That does sound like the deep end."

Lucy then told her about Gail's behavior and her visit to the house. "I don't know what to do with that. I know she's opposed to the relationship, but whether her antipathy will ease with time, who knows? I hate to be in the middle of a close father-daughter relationship. I haven't told Richard about the visit and am not sure I should."

"I don't know him, but from what you've said, I think you should tell him. This isn't about taking sides, but he needs to know."

Lucy nodded. "No secrets. I feel strongly about that."

"And how do you feel about him?"

"I care deeply for him. He's a lovely, kind man. It's more about me wondering if I'm ready."

"What are the signs that you're not ready?"

"Well, doing crazy things like the other night in his office."

"Hmm... Maybe not the best thing if you wanted to keep the relationship, and specifically your lovemaking, friendly. However, it doesn't sound crazy to me. Quite the contrary. There's obviously a strong attraction on both sides."

"When Gail stomped in, I felt like a teenager being chastised by the principal."

"I don't have to tell you that Gail's issues are about Gail, not you and not her father."

"Yes, but it does make things awkward and messy."

"Love and relationships can be messy, even the best ones."

"Then there's Rob. I think everything's settled and I've moved on, then I see him and completely unravel. I don't want to be with him, but it sometimes it feels familiar and comfortable. Does that make sense? I don't think things are too hunky dory with him and Chloe, so that's why he's coming around telling me he's made a mistake."

"Is that something you'd like to explore? Reconciliation?"

"Six months ago maybe. Now, no. It's over. I know it's over. Even if I wasn't seeing Richard, Rob and I will never be together again. Too much time, too much hurt."

"Have you made that clear to him?"

"Yes."

"Then your job is complete. The most important thing is to decide what *you* want. Not what Rob or Richard or Gail or anyone wants. Just you."

"I'm not sure how to do that. I've always been out there thinking about everyone else. The kids, my mom, Rob, my friends."

"Ah, the way of women, especially moms."

"Yes."

"Is it just physical with Richard, do you think?"

"No. I care deeply for him. If I'm being honest, the first time we met in Arizona, I fell hard, like a ton of bricks. Then I thought, this is crazy. I'm not much older than his kids. Maybe I'm searching for a father figure since our father was, and is, such a mess."

"Is that true, do you think?"

Lucy shrugged.

"Would you like to talk about your childhood and your relationship with your father?"

"Not especially. I'm sure Harriet's filled you in. If you met him, you'd think he was great. Back then, he was quiet, mild-mannered Dr. Jekyll by day and hideously cruel Mr. Hyde as soon as the cocktail hour rolled around. My mom took most of the abuse. We all pretended it wasn't happening. Dad's okay now, just kind of a broken-down mess, but no longer violent or nasty."

"Are you close to him?"

"Not especially. I have him to dinner every so often."

"You ever talk about the past?"

"Nope. He's apologized, but that's about as far as he goes. He's remarried, but still adores my mother and mourns her loss."

"Do you feel responsible for him and his well-being?"

Lucy stared at Elise, wondering how the conversation had turned to Judson Winthrop. "Rob and I used to fight about him."

"Oh?"

"He always took Mother's side and thought I shouldn't have anything to do with him. He's crazy about our mother."

"And now?"

"He still goes to see her occasionally, but not like when we were married."

"Does that feel okay to you?"

Lucy sighed. "Honestly, it's a bit weird, but Mother and I have talked about it. She's very reserved around him, but I see no reason for her to cut him off, and I've told her that. Rob is like a son to her. He's been really good to her over the years."

"A tangled web."

Lucy smiled. "Yes, compounded by living in a small town."

"So, does exploring your relationship with your father seem like something that would be useful at this point in your life?"

"Not really."

"Then what's next?"

"Move to the city, where no one knows me?"

Elise smiled. "Hmm... That's one option. How about brainstorming about how you can make it work here? Even if you eventually move to the city, you might give yourself a measure of peace?"

"Maybe."

"I think our time is up. Would you like to make another appointment?"

"Yes, please."

"Okay, in the meantime, I've got some homework for you. As often as you remember in situations with family, friends, Richard, Rob, whoever, take a minute to ask yourself, 'Does this bring me joy?'

and recognize and name whatever feeling arises. Would that be okay?"

Lucy nodded, tucking the appointment card in her bag. "Thanks, Elise."

"My pleasure. See you next week."

"So?' Lolly asked as she stepped into the office. She was alone.

"So nothing. Where's Wolfie?"

"At the post office. Was she helpful?"

"Yes, I think so."

"Maybe I'll try her.

"Uh-huh."

"That's all I'm gonna get, isn't it?" Lolly said as she taped up the last two boxes for shipping.

"Yup. There's really nothing to tell. I blurted out the whole, sad soap opera, she listened, asked a few questions, then gave me some homework."

"Homework?"

"Yes, I'm supposed to ask myself if situations and people bring me joy."

"Okay—so what about now? Am I bringing you joy?"

Lucy laughed as she threw a ball of brown wrapping paper at her partner. "You always bring me joy, dearie. Why do you think I went into business with you?"

"Aw...and here I thought it was my superior business acumen."

CHAPTER 19

Lucy loved Christmas Eve. Even with the roller-coaster emotional ride of the past few weeks, she smiled as she decorated and prepared foods for her neighborhood open house. The venue rotated, but this year was her turn to host. The house looked especially beautiful at Christmas with its laurels, boughs, and berries everywhere. As she hung the mistletoe over the doorway between the living and dining rooms, she remembered years past and how Rob would grab her in his arms and kiss her the minute it went up.

"Not this year," she said aloud. "Never again."

With the kids at Rob's for lunch and to exchange gifts, she was glad of the time to marshal her thoughts and complete last-minute preparations. The smell of cinnamon and cloves wafted in from the kitchen, and the piney scent of their enormous twinkling tree filled the family room. *I will miss this beautiful house*, she thought, *but it's time to talk about leaving.* She intended to have a family meeting about it, but kept putting it off. *Maybe it makes things too real?*

Her cell phone buzzed, and she ran to grab it from the front-hall table. "Hello?"

"Hi, it's me."

"Richard?"

"Yeah, this is the farm's office phone. My cell phone broke. Gail is out getting me a replacement. How are you?"

"Busy. Getting ready for tonight."

"Of course, I won't keep you. Just wanted to tell you we're looking forward to stopping by. Thanks for including us."

"Of course."

"Not sure who'll tag along, but I'll be there with bells on."

"Richard, if your family's together and enjoying the evening, don't push to come over here."

"I wouldn't miss it for the world."

"Is everyone home?"

"Everyone but Pam. She stayed in Maine. She's spending Christmas with her Aunt Cherie, Laura's sister. They're very close."

"Well, we'd love to have whoever would like to come."

"What's the rest of the day like for you?"

"Church at four thirty, then home and doors open."

"Do Amy and Rob go with you?"

"Usually, but they're at their dad's. I encouraged them to stay as he won't see them tomorrow. They'll be back in time for the party tonight."

"Would you like company at church? I'd love to go with you."

"I take my mom, but of course, if you'd like to come. But aren't you busy with your family?"

"Not that busy. I'll pick you up. What time?"

"Four. The Christmas Eve service fills up fast."

"Perfect. I'll see you at four."

Lucy smiled, shaking her head. *What will my family think of this?*

Helen was delighted. She liked Richard, and they talked amiably on the way to the meeting house at Harriet's school. They settled in on the thinly padded wooden pews, carols playing softly before the start of the service. As a tall woman rose to offer a reading, Richard reached over and took her hand. Lucy leaned against him, comforted and warmed by his nearness.

"So ladies," he said, as he dropped them back at Lucy's. "I'll be back with the gang in no time."

As mother and daughter walked arm in arm up Lucy's front walkway, Lucy carrying Helen's small overnight bag, it began to snow.

"A white Christmas after all," Helen said.

"Yes, the house looks lovely when it snows."

"That it does."

"I've decided I'm going to move out this year. If Amy and Rob are okay with it."

"Where will you go?"

"Not sure. Maybe rent a house for a while. I have a couple of leads. I could probably switch with Rob. I'm assuming he'll move back in here."

"What about Morgan's Fire?"

Lucy laughed, unlocking the front door. "Move in with Richard and his daughters? I don't think so."

"You're fond of him, though?"

"Yes."

"Maybe someday?"

"Maybe."

"I like him."

"Me too. Now let's get your bag upstairs, and then I've got to get the appetizers in the oven!"

CHAPTER 20

"Who of the Yarners is coming?" Helen asked as she, Amy, and Lucy made last-minute preparations. Rob and Wolfie had lit the fire and brought in plenty of logs. Now he and Wolfie were hiding in the den watching a football game. The Darn Yarners were Helen's group of eight women who met monthly to share writing, books, and occasionally crafts. Helen often claimed it was the Yarners who had saved her life when they moved to Horseshoe Crab Cove permanently.

"Well, your roommate, Frankie, of course," Lucy said. "And, Mavis. She and Lolly are coming sans Maisie, who's with her dad tonight. Rosa and family couldn't make it 'cause they're super busy at the restaurant. As you know the Childs sisters and families go to Cuttyhunk for Christmas. Belle said she and Will are coming along with Billy, but Sadie's still in France. In fact, speaking of the Pollarts, I see them coming up the walk. Rob—turn off the TV!" she called as Helen headed to the front door to greet them.

Belle and Will Pollart ran the docks and fisheries along with their son, Billy. Their daughter Sadie was an art restorer based in Boston who had been in residence at the Louvre for the past six months. When Helen had first moved to the village, she had worked in the Pollarts' fish market several days a week. It was Belle who invited her to join the Darn Yarners. The Pollarts lived on the southern shore in one of an enclave of houses owned mostly by African-Americans. The locals referred to it as "mini Oak Bluffs" after the town on Martha's Vineyard that was home to so many elite and wealthy African-Americans. Belle and Will were not rich, but some of their neighbors were.

"Merry Christmas!" Will said, his booming voice carrying through the house. Belle followed him in, a platter of shrimp in her arms. Billy and his live-in girlfriend, Aisha, brought up the rear. All four of them wore funny Christmas sweaters.

Belle handed the platter to Lucy, then hugged Helen. "Hey, girl, good to see you."

Short, petite, and slender, Belle had muscles of iron from years of manual labor. Her cropped salt-and-pepper hair framed a lovely oval face, her dark eyes always twinkling. She was dwarfed by her tall, broad-shouldered husband, his skin much darker than hers and without a single wrinkle even after a lifetime working outdoors. "Good genes," Belle always said when people asked how he could look so young. Shorter, Billy favored his mother, but had the strong, muscular frame of his father. Aisha was petite, dark, and willowy, dressed tonight in black velvet leggings and a crazy red tunic top featuring Rudolph with a large red pom-pom nose.

"You guys look great," Lucy said. "Get yourselves drinks. Wolfie or Rob can help. Here come the hordes." As she spoke, a number of neighbors streamed in. At the tail end came Frankie Brown, a local painter, Helen's fellow glass artist and erstwhile private investigator. Tall, with curly salt-and-pepper hair, Frankie had striking blue eyes. A solid, mostly calm presence, Frankie was Helen's best friend.

Pretty soon the party was in full swing, the house full of adults and teenagers. Small children ran from room to room, Rob and his friends chasing them. They still had some toys in the basement playroom, so Amy and her friends gathered the little ones and headed down.

As Lucy passed a platter of stuffed mushrooms, the front door opened and the Morgan family stepped in. "Welcome! Hello!" she called, pointing to the study. "Coats in there."

Ava and Dan had brought their kids. He held Laura, the two-year-old, and Sasha and Cameron stood next to their mother.

"Hi, kids," Lucy said, greeting them. "Amy and her friends are playing really cool games in the basement, if you'd like to join them?"

Richard caught her eye and smiled, a private, fleeting smile she liked to think was hers alone. He turned to his grandchildren. "I'll take 'em down. Come on, kids!"

Behind them, the rest of the Morgan siblings followed, even Gail.

Rich hugged Lucy. "You sure you want this many more bodies?"

She laughed, returning his embrace. "The more the merrier! Come in, come in. My son Rob's through there helping with drinks, as is Wolfie. There's pretty much anything you'd want, including bowls of eggnog and punch in the family room."

The Morgans were quickly swallowed up by the crowd of neighbors and villagers. Even Gail seemed to be engaged talking with Belle. As Lucy bent to take a sheet of crab puffs from the oven, Richard found her. "What a party!"

She smiled, wiping strands of hair from her brow. "Did you get the kids settled in?"

"They're in heaven. Me too. What a great way for my crew to meet some of the locals. Thanks so much for including us."

She touched his arm. "I'm really glad you're here."

"Wish we were alone."

"Well, we're not, and no sneaking off to the study tonight," she whispered.

His arm circled her waist, and he gave her ass a playful pat. "This would be the perfect time. No one would hear a thing with all this noise."

"Ha-ha. Once was enough!"

"Aw... Where's your spirit of adventure?" He bent and kissed her cheek. "Can I help with passing?"

"Wouldn't you rather mingle or be with your family?"

"I can mingle with those crab puffs and introduce myself along the way."

"Okay, then," she said, slipping the puffs onto two plates. "Thank you."

"Mmm, these smell good, but not as good as you," he whispered as he took the plates. "You look especially sexy tonight. In fact, my libido has gone into overdrive."

She gave him a wicked look. "Better check it if you're going to be in public. Do you need an apron?"

"I'll let you know," he said, pecking her cheek again as he slipped by her.

She couldn't help looking down. The front of his dark khakis was smooth. *Libido indeed!*

~

As the last of the guests departed, Rob, Helen, Wolfie, Amy, and Frankie cleaned up while Lucy stood at the door waving to her immediate neighbors, Betty and Kit Nelson. As they headed across the snow-covered lawn. Kit, who'd had too much to drink, leaned heavily on his wife.

"Be careful!" she called.

"No worries!" Betty called as they rounded a tall hedge and walked out of sight.

Lucy closed the door and leaned back, smiling. It had been a fun evening. Lots of work, but worth it. Richard and all his children and grandchildren seemed to enjoy themselves, and each had hugged her on their way out, even Gail. She doubted that anything would change with her relationship with Richard's prickly daughter, but she hoped Gail might have met some potential friends. There had been quite a number of guests her age.

"Penny for your thoughts," Frankie said as she passed by with empty plates and glasses.

Lucy smiled at her mother's dear friend. "It was fun, and it's over."

"'Twas fun. You're looking very well, by the way. Dating must suit you."

"Hmm... Don't know about that. Have you and Mom been talking?"

"Every morning."

"Gossips."

Frankie grinned. "And proud of it!"

"Here, let me take some of that," she said, reaching toward Frankie's precarious load.

"I got it, thanks. I have to say that I missed seeing that soon-to-be brother-in-law of yours. He's a handsome lad."

"Kyle? Yes, he's a great guy and gorgeous just like the rest of his family. Wait'll you see them all together. You're going to the wedding, right?"

"Wouldn't miss it for the world."

"Good."

"His uncle, your beau, ain't bad lookin' either."

Lucy blushed. "Yeah, he's nice looking."

"Better watch out. Every single woman was drooling over him tonight."

"Oh dear, poor Richard. Come on, let's get that stuff to the kitchen so you and Mum can put your feet up. Rob took your bag up to your room, right?"

Frankie winked. "I'm all set and ready for Santa." Like a beloved great aunt, Frankie had been staying overnight Christmas Eve for years.

"Oh, Frankie," Lucy said, her voice wistful. "Remember those days sprinkling reindeer food on the lawn and putting out milk and cookies for Santa?"

"Like it was yesterday. And I'll be sprinkling food on the lawn this year, don't you worry."

"Oh, Frankie, I love you."

"Back at you, kid."

CHAPTER 21

"So, that was really fun at Lucy's last night," Ava said as the Morgan family sat down to their traditional Christmas brunch. Callie had made eggs Benedict, and baskets of fresh muffins lined the table. Elegant Christmas wineglasses held fresh-squeezed orange juice. Everyone but Pam was there, even Wolfie, who sat between his niece and nephew, entertaining them with napkin folding.

"'Twas indeed," her father said. "Lucy's a wonderful hostess."

Ava nodded. "And she knows everyone. I met so many people I've been hearing about, like Mavis LaSalle. We've been trying to get a hold of her for months about using her shoreline for research."

"Do you actually need her permission?" Teddy asked.

Dan smiled at his brother-in-law. "No, but if we can't go across her land, that means a boat every time we want go out there because the shore on either side of her is impassable."

"Bummer," Teddy said, grabbing a huge cranberry orange muffin.

"Did you have fun, sweetie?" Richard asked, turning to Gail.

She shrugged. "It was okay."

"Seemed like you were in the middle of a lively crowd."

"Yup," Weezie said, raising her glass. "Gail and I were invited to a New Year's Eve party, weren't we, sis? I'm sure you guys can come if you're still around."

"Not the married old fogies?" Ava said.

Weezie laughed. "You too. It's at the Rodriguez farm. Raffi invited us, and he's got a lot of adorable friends."

"Better watch out for that one," Ava said. "He's got quite the reputation. According to village gossip, the expression 'love 'em and leave 'em' was made for him."

"His older brother, Sandy, Dad's old employee, sure gave Lolly the shaft," Wolfie said. All eyes turned to the youngest sibling, who rarely spoke a word at family dinner except to the children.

"Seemed like such a good kid the summer he spent with us in Maine," his father said.

"Well, he seems to have turned into a weasel since then," Wolfie said.

Ava nodded. "Broke my heart back in the day. I'm surprised since Lolly was coming that Lucy invited either brother."

"Lolly was cool with it. She's still close to some members of Sandy's family," Wolfie said.

Talk turned to the farm, then opening presents as Cameron and Sasha were clamoring to begin. Later, after the last gifts were opened, they took boxes of discarded paper and bows to the mudroom. Richard slipped out and went to his study. He loved his family, but could not get Lucy out of his mind. *Just need to hear her voice*, he told himself, *then my holiday is complete.*

She answered after several rings. "Merry Christmas!"

"Hi, how's it going over there?"

"Fine. Terrific. Winding down. We're all stuffed, Amy and Rob went off to see friends in the neighborhood, and Mom and Frankie are out walking. I'm just cleaning up, then I thought I'd go out to meet them or take a nap. Haven't decided which."

"Like some company for either activity?"

Lucy smiled. "Aren't you busy over there?"

"Not so much that I can't slip away for a half hour or so. I'd love to see you."

"When?"

"I can pop in the car in five."

"I'll get my woolies on and see you soon. Dress warmly."

THE TOWN OF SOMERS, WHERE LUCY LIVED, WAS ADJACENT TO Horseshoe Crab Cove, about eight miles from the peninsula and the village's main street. At the end of her street, miles of conservancy land, woods, and fields stretched all the way to the eighteen-mile Loop Trail that circled the village and peninsula. Walking trails were clearly marked, and at this time of year, they were popular with cross-country skiers and snowshoers.

Since she and Richard both wore boots, they decided to take the southern trail that led into the woods past several ponds. "I should have told you to bring snowshoes," she said.

"Left mine in Maine."

"You'll have to get some. These trails are great for it."

The sun warmed their cheeks as it peeked between the trees. Richard took her hand, and they walked in companionable silence for several minutes.

"This is lovely," he said softly.

"Yes."

"And so are you, dear Lucy."

She squeezed his hand. "Did you have a fun Christmas?"

"Yup. You?"

"Always."

"I think Wolfie wanted to run away to your house, but he stuck it out."

"Is he staying with you tonight?"

"Probably. He enjoys being with his brothers. And sisters."

"Gail looked like she was having fun last night."

"Yes, I think she did. Good for her to get out. Apparently, the movie-star-handsome Rodriguez boy has asked her and Weezie to a New Year's Eve affair."

Lucy smiled. "I've heard about those. The Grille stays open until after midnight, so while Rosa and Cesar aren't home, Raffi parties."

"Isn't he a little old for that?"

"Apparently not."

"Like my two, he still lives at home?"

"He travels a lot. He's an environmental attorney. Goes all over the country on projects. He specializes in wind and solar. Spark knows him. He built a barn and guest house on his parents' property, and that's where he stays when he's home. The barn's heated, and I'm guessing it's where the party will be."

"Sounds like an enterprising young man. Now, my girl, let's talk about something else."

"Like?"

"Like my Christmas present to you." They stood in a small clearing, flat boulders scattered around the perimeter. He pulled a long, narrow box from his jacket pocket.

"Oh, Richard! My gift for you is back at the house."

"No worries. You can still open mine. Come here and sit."

They sat side by side on a large, flat boulder as Lucy unwrapped his present to find a blue velvet jewelry box. She snapped it open, awestruck to find a sparkling bracelet of silver horseshoe crabs set with diamonds and emeralds. "Oh, Richard, it's beautiful and way too much!"

He smiled, taking her hand. "'Tis but a trinket. I'd give you the world if I could."

"Emeralds are my birthstone. Tell me these stones aren't real."

"A little birdie told me your birthday was in May. Want help putting it on?"

"Richard, I cannot accept this."

"Yes, you can. I'm loaded, in case you haven't heard."

"But where did you? I mean... I've never seen anything like it."

"I have an artist friend who works with precious stones. She made it for me." He helped her with the clasp.

Lucy held her arm out, admiring the delicate work. "It's the loveliest thing I've ever seen."

"Good!" he said, "I'm glad you like it."

"Should I take it off, do you think? I hate to risk losing it in the snow."

"It has a safety clasp. It'll be fine."

Lucy turned and circled her arms round his shoulders. "You are a wonderful man, Richard Morgan, and not just because you give me jewels."

He drew her closer, and their lips met, a deep kiss that expressed the longing and love they both felt for each other. He took one glove off and slipped his hand inside her jacket, caressing her cashmere sweater, fingers deftly moving the hem aside to find her soft skin as his hand moved upward to stroke and caress her breasts.

Lucy pulled back. "This is definitely *not* a good idea out here in the freezing cold."

"No, but it's a delicious thought, isn't it?" He gently massaged each breast, then withdrew his hand, smoothing her sweater down. "My cock is hard as a rock, so I may have trouble walking."

Lucy laughed, standing up, straightening her jacket and extending her hand. "Come on, tiger. I'll help you even though that bulge in your jeans is beyond tempting."

"Oh geez! Lucy Brennan, do you have any idea how much I want you right now?"

She gave him a mischievous look. "I'm afraid I do. The feeling is mutual, but we better head back before it gets dark."

As the trail ended, they kissed again, then walked the short distance to her house. "Come in. Your present is still under the tree."

Helen and Frankie were in the kitchen drinking hot cocoa as they arrived. Helen took one look at Lucy and said to her friend, "Remember the book I wanted to show you? Bring your cocoa, and we'll have a look. It's upstairs."

Lucy smiled at him. "Subtle, huh?"

"I love your mother."

"Here you go," she said, handing him her gift. "I'm afraid it's not a diamond-and-emerald bracelet."

"Thank goodness," he said, slowly unwrapping it.

"But it was made with love."

Lucy had knitted the soft green scarf, choosing the yarn carefully. As he wrapped it around his neck, she knew she had chosen well. It suited him.

"I love it, darling, thank you!" He pulled her close for a kiss just as the back door opened and Amy and Rob appeared.

Shortly after their arrival, Richard said his goodbyes and departed, saying he'd call soon. As she closed the door, Lucy gazed down at her wrist where the bracelet twinkled in the evening light.

"Merry Christmas," she whispered, tears rimming her eyes.

CHAPTER 22

"You're taking that one?" Lucy asked as Amy crammed a very skimpy bikini into her suitcase.

"Mom!"

"Have you packed plenty of sunscreen?"

"Yes, and I'm sure it's readily available on the ship." Their father was taking Amy and her brother on a weeklong Seabourn Caribbean cruise to celebrate the new year.

"And three times as expensive. What about cover-ups? Are you taking that pretty blue one we got last year?"

"Not unless I want to look like Granny Clampett." Recently they had been binge watching old episodes of *The Beverly Hillbillies*.

"Ha-ha. It makes you look very grown-up and sophisticated. Isn't that a good thing?" Lucy didn't want to say sexy.

"I've got it covered, Mom, excuse the pun. No worries."

"Seabourn is super fancy. I can't wait to hear about it," Lucy said, thinking, *we never took a trip like this when we were together.*

"According to Chloe, our cruise director, it's only fancy in amenities. They don't expect us to dress up."

A pang of sadness hit her, thinking about Chloe sharing the trip with their children. *Don't go there, Mom. You can fall apart after they depart.* "What time's your Dad coming?"

"Eleven."

"I'll miss you."

"Mom, what are you going to be doing? Have you made plans with friends or Mr. Morgan?"

"Not yet, but I'll be fine."

"Do something crazy with Aunt Lolly."

"She and her mom took Maisie to Disneyworld."

Amy sat down on the bed. "Are you sure this is okay? Do you want me to tell Dad I can't go?"

Lucy smiled at her beautiful daughter. Amy had been over-the-moon excited about the trip for months. "If I said *please, Amy, don't go,* that would be okay with you?"

Amy's face fell. "Are you serious?"

"Of course not. You go and have fun. Just not too much fun. And be wary of teenage boys on vacation. I wish one of your friends was going."

"We'll be fine. Isn't that your phone?"

Lucy hopped up and followed the ringing to her cell on the hall table. The number was unfamiliar. "Hello?"

"Lucy?"

"Yes."

"This is Gail Morgan."

Surprised, Lucy, sat on the stairs. "Hi, Gail, how are you?"

"Fine, thanks. And thank you for including us on Christmas Eve. It was fun."

"My pleasure."

"I was calling... Well, we wanted to know... Weezie and I were invited to the Rodriguezes' farm for New Year's Eve. Do you know them well?"

"Pretty well. Rosa, the mom, is a good friend of my mom's. They own the Cove Grille. Have you eaten there yet?"

"Yes, Dad took us to lunch there a couple of weeks ago. Anyway, what I... We were wondering is, do you think it'll be okay? I mean, are Raffi and his friends huge partiers? We're happy to party, but not if it's just a bunch of drunken yahoos."

Lucy smiled, taking a breath before she replied. "I think you'll be safe. Raffi's a good guy, and his friends are all professional people."

"That's what we thought, but just wanted to check. Well, thanks, then."

"You're welcome. Have fun."

"Who was that?" Amy asked as she came back into the bedroom.

"Gail Morgan wondering if they'd be walking into *Animal House* on New Year's Eve with Raffi and his friends."

Amy laughed. "I hope you told her yes." Her eyes grew wide and misty. "I just love Raffi."

"Much too old for you! And steer clear of any Raffis on the ship!"

"Don't worry, Luce," Rob said as he loaded suitcases into his SUV. "I'll watch them like a hawk."

She forced a smile. *Sure you will. I'm sure Chloe has plans for you that don't include kid watching.* "Where's Chlo?"

"Last-minute packing. She's gonna Uber to the airport and meet us."

Amy rolled her eyes and made a gagging motion behind her father's back.

"Be nice," he said, spying her reflection.

Amy hugged her. "Bye, Mom!"

"Have a good New Year," her son Rob said as they embraced.

"Happy New Year, Luce... Lucy," his father said, hugging her. "Wish you could join us."

"I think that'd be a little crowded," she said. "Have a great trip."

She waved, watching until the SUV disappeared at the end of the street before heading up the front walk. A wave of loneliness washed over her, and she sighed. *Everyone leaving home again.*

When she checked her phone, there was a text from Richard. *Can I have a date for New Year's Eve?*

She smiled, texting, *Lovely. Why don't we have dinner at my house?*

Perfect, came back instantly, with several heart emojis.

Two days to think of what I'll serve, she thought, heading in to change. She and Lolly were taking the week off, but she had to stop by the office to sort through the mail. Then she was meeting Lynn Manguilli for lunch. Lynn had called several days before Christmas wondering if they could meet for tea, and Lucy had suggested lunch at the Café. Back from Saguaro, Harriet had been meant to join them, but she and Kyle decided on a last-minute New Year's getaway to Cape Cod. Lucy and Lynn had decided to meet anyway.

CHAPTER 23

"How are you settling in?" Lucy asked Lynn as Milly the waitress poured waters.

"You ladies need a few minutes?" she asked.

"Yes please, thanks, Milly," Lucy said.

As Milly disappeared, Lynn leaned across the table. "Gus told me Milly's parents own the restaurant up the street. Why's she here and not there?"

"Paul and Josie Connors, the Café owners, are her uncle and aunt. Josie's Rosa's sister. And Milly, poor thing, works breakfast and lunch here and dinners at the Grille."

"That seems like a lot."

"It is, but it's Milly's choice. She's saving money for her 'big adventure,' about which she will tell no one. She's an independent soul, our Milly."

"To answer your question, I'm doing okay. Just feeling a bit like a fish out of water."

"Such a big change for all of you. Where are the kids today?"

"Gus took them to the farm. Weezie offered to watch them. I'll swing by and grab them after lunch."

"How's your mom?"

"Holding her own. Chemo's taken a lot out of her, but she's a fighter. My dad's been taking her back and forth to New Haven."

Milly returned, pad in hand with two lemonades.

"So nice to meet you, Milly," Lynn said. "I've heard a lot about you from Gus."

Milly gave her a dimpled smile. "Love Mr. Casey! He's the nicest guy. You're lucky."

"Yes, I am."

They both ordered Cobb salads, and Milly flew off with a "Be right out!"

"Is there anything I can help with? Settling in? Unpacking?" Lucy asked.

Lynn's eyes filled with tears, and she brushed them away with the back of her hand. "Sorry. I seem to be doing a lot of this these days."

"Understandable."

"It's just so hard. I feel ridiculous saying that because I have the most wonderful fiancé in the world, two incredible kids, and a baby on the way."

Lucy smiled as she reached over to pat Lynn's hand. "Hormones may be the culprit?"

"Maybe. I knew who I was in the Valley, you know? I had a great job working with my dearest friend. Plus we were surrounded by support from Spark, the Morgans, and the Valley Stables guys. It's like I've been wrenched from the bosom of my family to live in a foreign country, present company excluded, of course. I'm so grateful to have you and Harriet and Kyle."

"There are Morgans on this coast too."

Lynn paused as if wondering if she should say more, then shrugged. "Richard's been wonderful, of course. He's as generous and giving as his brother. Oh my goodness, we want for nothing."

"But the rest of the family takes a bit of getting used to?" Lucy asked, eyes warm.

"Yes. Especially Weezie. I mean, I know I'm hormonal and all, but it's... She's... Well, she still hangs on Gus, flirts with him, even when I'm standing right there."

Lucy smiled. "That's Weezie, I'm afraid. She's a force of nature."

"A gorgeous one too."

"As are you. Can't Gus speak to her?"

"He has. Several times."

"Confession? I have my own issues with the Morgans," Lucy said, and gave her a brief summary of her interactions with Gail.

"You're kidding," Lynn said as she finished.

"Nope. Gail has made it very clear that she does not approve of me and will fight any close relationship to her dad."

Lynn gazed over, her charcoal eyes wide. "What does Richard say?"

"He says to just ignore it and she'll get used to the situation."

"Does he know she paid you a visit?"

"No. Not yet."

"What's the matter with her?"

"Needs a life of her own, I suspect," Lucy said as Milly delivered their salads and a basket of warm crusty bread. "Thanks, Mill."

"Can I get you anything else?"

"Thanks, I think we're set." Lucy turned to Lynn and raised her glass. "Here's to a united front. We will not be defeated by the Morgan girls."

Lynn giggled. "You're right, they are a force, aren't they?"

"As are all the Morgans, except maybe Wolfie. What a sweetheart he is. Probably why he's living at my house."

"Your Richard's no minor force himself."

"You're right about that. Lynn, would you like me to speak to him about Weezie? He might be able to warn her off."

"No, but thanks. That might make things worse. She doesn't seem to listen to her father."

"What does Gus say?"

"To ignore it and that he has it under control."

"Which I'm sure he does. Weezie's just showing off."

"I have something else I wanted to ask about. We were going to have the wedding in Connecticut at my mom's, but now we're thinking it's too much for her and we should have it here. Very small.

My family, the Morgans, I guess—" Lynn made a face "—and Gus's family from Wyoming. Polly and Kevin are coming too. It's about fifty, maybe sixty people tops. Do you have a suggestion as to a venue? Richard offered to have it at the farm, but I would rather not."

"Have you been out to the Cove? Mavis LaSalle's estate? It's gorgeous."

"And very expensive, I'm sure. My parents offered to cover costs, but I hate to ask them to spend a small fortune right now."

"Mavis is our mother's good friend. I could call her for you. See what she might be able to offer. It's her off season, and this is technically her vacation time, but when she, Lolly, and Maisie get back from Disneyworld, maybe we could take a drive over? When were you thinking?"

"End of January? I know, it's crazy trying to plan a wedding on such short notice, but I want to be married before the baby comes."

"Maybe not. Mavis might be persuaded to do it for a friend. I'll give her a call when I get home."

"Thank you so much."

"I'd say we could do it at my house, but it's a little chilly for a tent in the backyard."

Lynn smiled, then her eyes darkened. "I'm really scared. Is that normal?"

"Scared of getting married?"

"No, of having the baby. The delivery. Gus's wife died in childbirth or shortly after, and he's scared too."

"Have you shared that with your OB?"

"Yes, and she's been great. I can't seem to shake it, though."

"Who's your birthing coach? Gus?"

"He'll be there, and Polly wants to come, but it's really hard to gauge, especially since she'd have to leave the Cottage and the kids twice in a little over a month. My sister Barb's offered too."

"Gus will be a great coach," Lucy said, thinking back to her deliveries and how amazing Rob had been through both births. "You might find that it's best with just the two of you."

Lynn nodded. "Honestly, I'd prefer that. We're not sure what to do about the kids."

"Put me on speed dial. I will be happy to come and stay with them when you're ready to go to the hospital."

"That's incredibly kind of you. Are you sure? Weezie offered, but I'd much rather leave them with you."

"I'd be honored. I can stay at your house with them or bring them back to mine. Amy and Rob would love to have them."

"They had such a good time with your guys on Christmas Eve."

"We'd love it. How's your salad?"

"Delicious."

"Good," Lucy said, smiling. "It's going to be okay, Lynn. And if you'd like to talk to someone, either you, Gus, or both of you, Elise Nolan in town is a wonderful therapist. I just went to see her for the first time last week, but Harriet's been with her for years."

"I'd love her contact information."

"And someday, when you're ready, you'll find your place here—jobs, friends, whatever. Lolly and I are always looking for extra people, and we don't know how long we'll be able to keep Wolfie. Richard wants him to run the vineyard. I know Merlin's Closet is not the same as the Cottage, but we have a good time."

Lynn gazed at her, tears in her eyes again. "No worries, these are happy tears. I was wrong. We haven't left family and kindness behind."

"No, you haven't. There are some prickly pears around, but I think you'll find another family in the Cove. That was certainly the case for us when Mum moved us here permanently. Her Darn Yarners embraced us from day one, and they've never let go."

That's why I'm going to be all right, Lucy mused as they strolled down the sidewalk to their cars. *This loving community will make sure of it.*

CHAPTER 24

"This is lovely," Richard said, gesturing to the small table Lucy had set for their dinner by the fire.

"Cozier. No sense peering at one another across the big table."

"I agree. You look especially pretty tonight. Pink suits you."

She smiled, glad she had chosen her favorite sweater rather than wearing something perhaps sexier. "It's mauve."

"Well, whatever it is, it's perfect, as are you."

"You are going to have to take off those rose-colored glasses, Richard Morgan. I am far from perfect."

"To me you are," he said, drawing her into his arms. "I missed you this week. See how much?"

As his body pressed against hers, she felt him growing hard. "Hmm…that feels good. Can I get you something to drink?"

"I'd rather make love to you first."

"Well, it might mean the mauve sweater disappears," she said, slipping it over her head and tossing it on the sofa. They were standing in the family room, huge glass windows open to the backyard, no shades.

"Can your neighbors see us?"

"Not unless they're peeking through the thirty-foot arborvitae. They're pretty thick."

"Well...in that case..." He hesitated, then pulled her close, hands everywhere.

Lucy arched her body, rubbing against him. "But, you never know who might be cutting through our backyard. Come on, my sexy exhibitionist."

"Look who's talking," he said, allowing her to lead him to the stairway. On every step, they kissed, clothes falling all around them until they reached the second-floor landing, both naked and suffused with warmth and desire. Richard cupped her full, round breasts, his lips and tongue teasing, licking, gently sucking as her nipples grew hard.

Lucy stroked him, her hands moving in a delicious rhythm even as she ached for his stiff, throbbing cock inside her. Richard panted as his mouth found hers in a deep, hungry kiss. Voice husky with desire, he kissed her ear, whispering, "I'd take you here against the wall if I didn't want to fuck you on that big beautiful bed ahead of us. Whatta ya say, baby?"

Lucy smiled, releasing him, arms circling his neck. "I say, what are we waiting for?"

"Not sure I'll make it," he said, "but I'm sure gonna try." Richard swept her up in his strong arms and carried her to the bed, then laid her down gently. For a few seconds, he stood over her. "Beautiful." Then gently he spread her legs apart, easing himself onto the edge of the bed, poised above her. "What do you want, my sweet girl?"

"I want you inside me, taking me to the moon and back."

He smiled the way he had the first time they met. A warm, genuine, soul-piercing smile that lit up his dark eyes. "You have no idea how happy that makes me."

"I just might," she said, stroking him again, then taking the condom from him and slipping it on him. "How long has this been in your hand?"

"Since I threw my pants over the bannister." He leaned down, kissing her as his hips dropped and he moved between her legs. Lucy arched up, her warm, wet depths welcoming him.

"Geez," he groaned as he plunged deep. "Oh baby!"

They moved gently at first, then harder, faster, more urgently, as if their lives depended on every delicious thrust, every agonizing withdrawal. Lucy's fingers dug into his shoulders, and for a brief time, she wondered if she could hold on to sanity. Every fiber of her being writhed in sweet ecstasy as they rose to a crashing climax. In her mind, she was screaming, but she wasn't sure if he could hear her.

As their ardor subsided, they collapsed into each other's arms. Richard pulled her close and rolled onto his side, still maintaining their sweet connection.

"Happy New Year," he whispered, trailing kisses down her neck.

"You hungry?"

"For you."

"Hmm... Let's have dinner, and then we have all night."

"I like the sound of that. You stay put, and I'll gather all the clothes."

Lucy threw a quilt over herself as she watched him cross the room. For a man his age—any age, for that matter—Richard was in great shape. Hard ass, strong legs, and back, a spring to every step. He returned shortly with an armful of clothing, and they dressed side by side. *Would I want to be doing this every day?*

"What are we having?" he asked as they headed downstairs. "Something smelled amazing when I stepped into the house."

"Cioppino."

"Ah, the favorite dish of every virile Italian fisherman."

Lucy laughed. "Something like that. It's mostly a nice broth that you can throw any kind of seafood into, and it tastes great."

"Mmm, so do you."

"What can I get you to drink?"

"Red wine? I brought some. It's on the counter."

"Why don't you uncork it, and I'll get things ready?"

They lingered by the fire, enjoying the savory stew, crusty bread, and arugula and fennel salad. Lucy had made chocolate pots au crème for dessert, which she served with a dollop of whipped cream. As they finished dessert, she opened a bottle of champagne. "Shall we adjourn to more comfortable seating?" she asked, pouring them each a glass.

"In a minute. Sit, darling," he said, eyes soft as he raised his glass. "To you."

"And you."

"To us."

Lucy nodded. "Yes."

Richard set down his glass and slipped from his chair onto his knee, reaching into his pocket for a small round box. As he moved, Lucy stared, knowing what was coming and wondering how she could stop it.

Before she could make a move, he said, "Lucy Winthrop, as I'm sure is pretty obvious, I love you. I never thought I'd say that to another woman. I feel incredibly lucky to have found you and—"

"Richard, wait."

He reached up, fingers to her lips. "Please, my love, let me finish. I've reached the place where I cannot imagine life without you. Wherever you are is home, and that's where I want to be. Lucy, please make me the happiest man alive and marry me." He opened the box to reveal a sparking emerald surrounded by diamonds.

"Richard... I..."

"If you'd rather have a traditional diamond, I can get that too."

"The ring is beautiful."

"Good. So what do you say, my beautiful girl?"

"Richard, I can't. I'm so sorry. I can't marry you. I'm not ready. I'm still finding my way."

He took both her hands in his. "We can find our way together."

She shook her head. "I'm sorry. I care very deeply for you, but I can't."

"I don't understand. What have we been doing the last few months? What about tonight? What was that?"

"It was incredible."

"Incredible sex?"

"No, much more."

He grasped the table to brace himself, then stood and slipped back into his chair. "I don't understand."

"I know. I'm not sure I do either, but I need to listen to myself, and myself is saying no."

"Yipes, I don't know what to say."

Lucy's heart ached as she watched him. He looked so dejected. "Want to sit on the sofa where it's more comfortable?"

"No, thanks." He snapped the box closed and pocketed it. "You know, I'm kind of tired. I think I'll head home. I've never been much of a stay-up-till-midnight guy."

"Oh, Richard, please don't go away mad."

"No worries," he said, reaching over to cup her chin. "Just weary and feeling my age, I guess. Or maybe just rusty at this courting thing. Can I help you clean up before I go?"

"No, I'm fine."

She watched as he grabbed his coat and pulled on his scarf. She wanted to say something, anything to ease the tension, but she couldn't form the words.

"Okay, then. Thank you for a delicious dinner and a lovely evening. Happy New Year, Lucy." He kissed her lightly, then opened the front door.

"Happy New Year," she said as he turned away and headed for his car. *What have I done? Oh, what have I done?*

CHAPTER 25

Kyle Morgan set a brown leather medical bag on the mudroom shelf. "Hey, Lucy, where's your sister?"

"Just showering. I'm early. How are you?"

"Great. Busy. It's been kind of nonstop between town and Morgan's Fire. How're you doing? Kids back?"

"Tomorrow."

"Hey, honey," he said, smiling as Harriet appeared, her hair damp.

She hugged him, returning his kiss. "Hi yourself. Long day?"

"Something like that. I'm gonna shower, then I'm happy to help out."

"We've got it covered," Lucy said. "Takeout from the Grille."

"Now you're talkin'." He headed for their bedroom, closing the door behind him.

"Your fiancé is a real sweetheart."

"Yes, he is."

"Have you decided on a date?"

Harriet made a face. "Do you really want to talk about this now? With everything you're going through?"

Lucy waved her hand. "My soap opera has nothing to do with your happiness. I can't wait for the wedding. I'm already dreaming of all the spa treatments I'm going to have. Not to mention those incredible meals that go on forever."

"We just decided. December twenty-eighth."

"Oh, so long to wait! Why then?"

"We want to be there for Ben and Leonora's anniversary party New Year's Day. This way we can combine the two, and hopefully everyone will stay on for both."

"What about your honeymoon?"

"We'll go right after New Year's. They can get a substitute for me for the week. Kyle's the one who'll be most missed."

"It's gonna be so fun!"

"Wine?"

"Love it."

"Red or white?"

"Whatever you're having."

"I was thinking of opening a bottle of Chianti to go with Cesar's lasagna."

"Good choice."

"How was your trip?"

"Fabulous, both of them. Too quick the visit to the Valley. We should have stayed there through New Year's. The Cape was lovely and quiet. So? Tell me about *your* New Year's Eve."

"Well, it started out great till he dropped his bombshell." She related highlights of their dinner, ending with "It was awful."

"I'm not sure I'd call a marriage proposal a bombshell."

"A surprise, then. Total shock."

"Why shocking? You'd have to be blind not to see how crazy Richard is about you."

"I know, and I'm pretty crazy about him."

"Then what's the problem?"

"I feel like I'm jumping into another relationship when I'm still not totally out of the last one."

"Rob? You're not considering going back to him?"

"No."

"That's good." Of all her family, Harriet harbored the strongest feelings about Rob, bordering on hatred. When a family function meant they had to be in the same place, she studiously avoided him as best she could, often asking Kyle to run interference.

"You know, you don't have to hate him for my sake."

"No worries there. I hate him for my own sake, thank you." She raised her glass and clinked Lucy's.

"So what smells so good?" Kyle asked, grabbing a beer from the fridge. Dressed in sweats, he wore thick wool socks and no shoes. He flashed one of the brilliant Morgan smiles, and Lucy was reminded of Richard and Wolfie.

"Cesar's lasagna."

"Great. You two having a private powwow?"

"Absolutely not!" Lucy said. "Sit, please."

He joined them at the kitchen table, grabbing a fistful of nuts from the bowl Harriet had set out. "What's new with two of my favorite women?"

Rather than ignore the elephant in the room, Lucy said, "We were discussing your wedding date and my soap opera life."

"Wedding's gonna be great," he said, clinking his beer bottle against their wineglasses. "And sorry about the proposal snafu. Uncle Dick's been moping around for the past few days, barking at everyone."

Lucy sighed. "Oh dear, he told you then."

"He'll get over it. You know, men like him and my dad and Spark, they're used to getting their way. People rarely say no to them. I mean, I'm talking about business, but that attitude can spill over into one's personal life."

"Maybe," Lucy said. "But I still feel like a shit. He's a wonderful man, and it was probably crazy of me to say no."

"No, it wasn't," Harriet said. "You know your heart."

"Do I?"

As she drove home that night, Lucy wondered, *Will I ever again have a clear sense of what my heart wants? Or did Rob Brennan take that away from me forever?*

~

"WHAT'S WRONG, DAD?" WEEZIE ASKED FOR THE FOURTH TIME THAT day. "If you won't tell us, at least get some professional help." They were cleaning up after supper, Gail washing and Richard and her sister drying and shelving.

"I'll be fine. Just processing, as Dr. Jenkins used to say." Jenkins had been their family physician in Maine. He had helped him pick up the pieces after Laura's death. It was Jenkins who found Linda, the nanny who'd lived with them until Wolfie left for college. Richard had assured Linda that she would always have a home with them and had given her a substantial settlement as she went off on her own. In her late forties now, she had moved to California to live with her sister, but she kept in touch.

"They have therapists in the village or Providence, if you're depressed," Weezie said.

Gail handed him a large platter. "It's Lucy, isn't it? This is why I thought that was a bad idea."

"What's wrong with Lucy?" Weezie said. "I like her. After all, we're going to be kind of family soon when Harriet marries Kyle."

Gail rolled her eyes. "Hardly."

"Stop, you two. She said no, that's all."

Gail gave him a sharp look. "What are you talking about?"

"No!" Weezie said, eyes wide. "You didn't, did you?"

"Yup."

"When, where?"

"New Year's Eve."

Hands on hips, Gail watched them, frowning. "Did what on New Year's Eve?"

"He proposed to Lucy, your ninny! That's so exciting, Dad! But, why did she say no? I'm pretty sure she's as crazy about you as you are her."

"Apparently not."

"What did she say? What reason did she give?" Weezie asked.

"It's complicated, but I think she doesn't feel she's ready, after her divorce and all. It hasn't been that long."

Weezie shook her head. "Plus he's always around, bothering her."

Gail untied her apron and sat at the kitchen counter. "Well, I for one think Lucy made a very wise decision. No sense rushing into anything. Why, you've only known each other for a short time."

"A year in June," he said.

Weezie hugged her father. "The thing to do is not to give up. She'll get there. Give her some space. Maybe not see her for a few weeks or so. Let her figure things out."

"For once, I agree with Weezie," Gail said. "I'm taking my book and going up."

"Now?" her sister said. It was quarter to eight.

"Yes, now. It's a great mystery, and I'm right at the good part."

"You know, Lucy's company specializes in esoteric, hard-to-find mysteries. You should ask her for recommendations," Weezie said.

"How would you know that?" her sister asked.

"Wolfie told me."

"Night, Dad," Gail said.

He hugged her. "Night, baby. And mum's the word on this proposal business for now, okay? I told Kyle and your brother 'cause I needed buddies to talk to, but no one else."

"No one outside the family, you mean?" Weezie asked.

"Inside and outside. Wolfie's with her every day. I don't want to interfere with their working relationship."

Weezie smiled. "He'd probably take Lucy's side."

"More than likely," he said. "What are you doing tonight, baby?"

"I'm going to Sara's yoga class, then maybe having a drink with her."

"I've got to ask Sara about her senior classes," he said.

"You are *many* years from being a senior, Dad!" Weezie said as she grabbed her jacket and yoga mat from the mud room.

Not so many, he thought as his daughters went their separate ways. *I feel about a hundred tonight.*

CHAPTER 26

Lucy and Amy sat in the kitchen, remains of a late breakfast in front of them. "So, I'm off to pick up Lynn. You want to come out to the Cove with us?"

"No, thanks. Much as I love Auntie Mavis, I've got a ton of stuff to do before Monday."

"Like unpack and finally wash your travel clothes? You've been back four days now. They must be very ripe."

Lucy and Rob had made laundry one of the kids' responsibilities from an early age. They'd even installed an extra washer and dryer unit in their shared bath. Then Lucy had learned to close her eyes when the piles built up.

"I will, I will," Amy said, waving her hand dismissively.

"We'll probably have lunch in town on our way back. Can I bring you something?"

"No, thanks. A couple of the girls are stopping by. We're gonna walk down for pizza."

"In between laundry loads? Later sweetie!"

~

"Mavis is a bit eccentric, but she's awesome at what she does," Lucy said as they drove up the long drive to Mavis's estate.

"This is amazing," Lynn said as she gazed at the open fields leading up to the main house.

"That's Netherfield Manor straight ahead," Lucy said.

"Someone's a Jane Austen fan. Why not Netherfield Park?"

Lucy chuckled. "Mavis likes to think she's being original. She's mad for Austen and a bunch of other authors. She's always emulating some flamboyant character from literature or film."

"Why not Pemberley, then?"

"Netherfield's more subtle, according to Mavis. It used to be Sheffington Manor. It's the original house on the estate that once included all of the peninsula. Mavis likes to put her stamp on things, so she renamed it. She lives in the big house. There are a couple of smaller function rooms there that might be perfect for you. Most of the big weddings are held in one of those two barns, or sometimes tents."

"This looks pricey," Lynn said. "I mean, my parents can afford it, but I hate to ask them, especially right now."

"Let's just see what she says. At the very least, we can pick her brain. She loves brainstorming about the perfect wedding. And she has a huge library of wedding books and resources."

Lucy parked alongside the house. As they approached the front door, it swung open. "Welcome, welcome, ladies!" Mavis called, a jaunty orange boa round her neck.

"Still in her Isadora Duncan phase," Lucy whispered as she waved to their host.

Mavis led them to a large, lavishly furnished library with thousands of pristine leather-bound books lining three walls, a wall of windows facing the water, and thick Persian rugs on the floor.

"Would you ladies like tea? Or water? Or really anything you'd like." She gestured to a sideboard in the corner.

"Water's fine," Lucy said. "Lynn?"

"That would be great, thanks."

"Sit. I'll get it," Lucy said. "Mavis?"

"Nothing for me, dear. I've already had gallons of coffee, and it's not even eleven." She waved Lynn to one of several buttery leather sofas, and she then sat beside her.

Once Lucy sat, water in hand, Mavis said, "Now then, let's hear about this wedding. Of course you can have it here with the Darn Yarners' discount, sixty percent off." She raised her hands. "No arguments."

"That's incredibly generous of you, Ms. LaSalle."

"Of course, you're family. And it's Mavis, please!"

They spent several hours talking and touring the grounds. Once back inside, Mavis asked, "Did one of the spaces speak to you?"

Lynn smiled. "I loved them all, but I think we'd be lost in the barns."

"My thoughts exactly," their host said. "Let's go back to the library and chat a bit more. I'd love to see you in the Persimmon. It's just the right size, and the buffets could be in the side parlor, bars at either end of the hall. What do you think?"

"The Persimmon is lovely," Lynn said. "Lucy, what do you think?"

"My favorite too."

Mavis clapped her hands. "Persimmon it is! Now you'll have to decide how much you want to be involved. I have all your ideas in the notebook I started today," she said, waving her iPad, where she'd been scribbling notes as they talked. "We can do everything or collaborate with anybody you'd like to bring in. Kendall, my chef, is extraordinary. Usually, she's part of the package, but since you're family, if you want to bring in your own caterer, that would be fine."

Lynn swallowed, looking from one to the other. "If it's not too much, I would love Kendall to do the food. My mom has a baker in Groton doing the cake."

"Music?"

"I hear your daughter's group is terrific."

Mavis frowned as Lucy gave Lynn a thumbs-up. "Hmm... If you like that kind of music."

"Which we do."

"I'll check with Marla, then. Will you need accommodations for anyone?"

"Yes, my family and Gus's. We're scrambling a bit on that."

"Well, scramble no more. Two of the cottages are available that weekend. They each have three bedrooms. Will that be enough? If not, there's space here in the house."

"More than enough, but are you sure?"

"Absolutely! Darn Yarner discount!"

"And I have two spare rooms, if you need them," Lucy said. "Maybe Polly and her family, if they come?"

Tears filled Lynn's eyes. "Thank you. You are both so incredibly kind and generous. Gus and I are so grateful."

"This is the Cove, dear. We take care of family here, don't we, Lucy?"

Lucy nodded.

She winked at Lucy. "Of course, when family members act like horse's asses, we may be forced to give them the boot."

Lucy knew Mavis was talking about Rob and Sandy, but she had no wish to discuss either.

"Sorry about the tears," Lynn said, wiping her eyes. "I seem to cry at the drop of a hat these days."

Seated beside her on one of the library sofas, Mavis leaned forward and patted Lynn's knee. "No worries. Totally understandable, my dear girl, in your condition. And Lucy tells me your mother's not well. Anyone would feel weepy at a time like this. You just leave all the arrangements to me. I promise to make your special day a happy, beautiful affair."

They drove back into town armed with a stack of wedding resources and the wedding journal Mavis had given Lynn. "What about a late lunch?" Lucy asked as they drove down Main Street.

"Thanks, but if it's okay with you, I'd like to get home and take a little nap. Gus took the kids to the farm, but they should be back soon."

"You okay?" Lucy asked as she turned down the road to their rental cottage.

"Yes, thank you so much. I don't know what I'd do without you."

"My pleasure. And please use my house for guests. Mother also has two rooms, and Harriet too. I know they'd be delighted."

"Richard offered as well," Lynn said. "He also offered to host the rehearsal dinner the night before, but the Caseys want to do it at a restaurant. Gus is handling that."

"Ballard's is nice. About ten miles up the coast. Not sure how many you're expecting, but they have a really pretty function room off the main dining room. Great food too."

"He's got his heart set on barbecue, poor guy. Where in the world will we find good barbecue?"

"Believe it or not, Salters Clambakes does cookouts and barbecues too. And their pork roasts and ribs are to die for." Lucy pulled into the driveway. "I'll text you the number when I get home. If you're thinking barbecue, have him check the availability of the American Legion Hall in town. It's perfect for that."

"Thanks."

"You okay?"

"Just nervous. Among everything else, there's Gus's promise to Dulcie and Cal's mom not to marry again. I keep worrying that he's gonna wake up one morning and tell me this has all been a huge mistake."

Lucy reached over and squeezed her hand. "Never. Gus loves you, and everything's going to be great. If you're okay with it, I'd give Mavis all your ideas, then let her run with it. It'll save you a lot of headaches, and she'll do an amazing job."

"I'm definitely okay with it. I can plan lessons and develop curriculum, but wedding planning is definitely not my forte. As soon as I clear things with Gus, Mavis gets carte blanche!"

"That's the spirit! I'll be in touch."

As Lucy drove back through town, she realized how unsettled and sad she'd felt when Lynn mentioned Richard. She hadn't heard a word from him since New Year's Eve. *What have I done?* she wondered for the hundredth time.

CHAPTER 27

The third week of the new year, Lucy worked alone in the office. Lolly and Wolfie were out delivering books. A knock at the door startled her, and she called, "It's unlocked!" The door opened, and she gazed up, surprised to see Gail Morgan.

"May I come in?"

"Of course. Wolfie's out, if you're looking for him?"

"No, it's you I came to see."

"Okay. Welcome to chaos. It's book fair season, and we're a bit overwhelmed and understaffed. Take a seat if you can find one."

Gail moved file folders off a swivel chair and sat. "Weezie tells me your catalogue features interesting mysteries."

Lucy nodded, unearthing the latest issue of *Merlin's Closet* from a pile on her desk and handing it to Gail. "Here you go. Hot off the press. My partner and I love mysteries. We try to find unusual ones. We're featuring a wonderful Irish writer this month, Cora Harrison. Her Burren mysteries are particularly delightful. Some are hard to find, but they're worth it."

"Thanks," Gail said, sliding the catalogue into her large purse.

"Is that why you're here? Reading suggestions?"

"No. I'm here because I have behaved like a twenty-six-year-old spoiled brat. Not to mention a petulant rude bitch, and a host of other unflattering descriptors. I'm here because I want to apologize and tell you I was wrong."

"You love your father and were being protective."

"No, I wasn't. I was scared."

"Of?"

"Losing him and losing my place in the house. I'm kind of pathetic, in case you haven't noticed. I mean, I'm good at my job and will promote the hell out of the farm and vineyard once things get off the ground, but I'm pretty hopeless when it comes to my personal life. Basically, I don't have one."

"But you will. There are lots of people your age in the village. You'll be surprised."

"I met... I mean, we, Weezie, and I met quite a few New Year's Eve at the Rodriguezes'."

"Oh, how was that? I hear it's quite the blast."

"It was fun and not too rowdy. I was surprised. I met a couple of the Millers. Karen and her brothers, Brick and Tim."

"Great people. Karen's my sister Harriet's best friend."

"She told me. What about Tim? Do you know him well?"

Lucy smiled. *Oh boy, she's met the village's version of Heathcliff.* "Yes, Tim's a great guy. Son of one of my grandmother's good friends, Faith. They're both Darn Yarners. Have you heard about that group?"

"Yes, Dad told us. Can't remember why he got on the subject."

"How is he? Your dad?" Lucy hadn't heard a word from Richard in three weeks. She missed him terribly. She was diligently meeting with Elise once, sometimes twice, a week, endeavoring to untangle her emotions.

"That's actually why I'm here. He's miserable."

"I'm sorry."

"Sorry enough to put him out of his misery?"

"So he told you about the proposal?"

"Only Rich, Weezie, and me. The others don't know, and he's asked us not to say anything, especially to Wolfie."

"Well, he'll be back soon, so we better talk fast. I haven't heard from your father since New Year's, and I haven't wanted to contact him because right now I can't give him what he wants."

"Why not? You love him. I know you do."

Lucy nodded. "Yes, I do. I just need some time on my own to sort things through. It's hard to explain, but I'm sure it's the right decision for me and your dad."

"Well, I just wanted to tell you I'm sorry and that if I had anything to do with pushing you away, I apologize."

Lucy leaned forward and squeezed her hand. "You did nothing. It's all me, and I'm very sorry for causing your dad distress. Saying no to him was one of the hardest things I've ever done."

Gail smiled. "Our dad's not used to hearing that word."

"You're not the first person to tell me that."

"'Cause it's true."

"Thanks for stopping by. Want a cup of tea?"

Gail stood up. "Thanks, but no. I think I'll head out before Wolfie gets back. Let you get back to work."

"If something catches your interest in the catalogue, let us know, and we'll order it for you. Family discount."

"Thanks."

As Gail turned the doorknob, Lucy said, "Tim Miller's a fisherman, but he also makes exquisite furniture, in case you're looking for something for the farm or a wedding present."

"Great idea!"

"His woodshop's not far from here. He shares a barn with Cooper Merrick, a blacksmith. Three blocks down, behind Corey's Hardware."

"Sounds good," Gail said, smiling as she closed the door behind her.

After Gail's departure, Lucy sat back, wondering what to make of the young woman's startling appearance. She felt certain that concern for her father had been the main catalyst for Gail's visit, but she smiled, thinking that handsome Tim Miller, who really did look like Lucy's vision of Heathcliff, may have figured into Gail's pop-in and perhaps her change of heart. *Happiness and hope are very powerful motivators*, she thought, closing her eyes for a five-minute cat nap.

"WHERE HAVE YOU BEEN?" RICH MORGAN ASKED AS HIS SISTER appeared at the dining room door.

"I was in town," Gail said, a red blush playing across her freckled cheeks.

"Doing...?" her brother asked.

"Errands, why?"

"We had a meeting with Zeke Ravensbrook to discuss the label and marketing."

"That was supposed to be tomorrow," Gail said, looking from her father to Rich. "And both Weezie and Wolfie were supposed to be here."

"They were, honey," Richard said. "Come, sit, all's well. We'll fill you in."

Gail sat, shrugging out of her coat. "Sorry, Dad."

"No problem. There will be many more meetings with Zeke in the weeks and months ahead. Rich, fill her in. I'm gonna get something to eat. Anyone want a sandwich?"

As he left the room, Richard wondered where his daughter had been. It wasn't like her to be absentminded." *Maybe we should have stayed in Maine,* he thought, not for the first time in the past few weeks. *No! Morgan, you can do this. At least I'll make a start, get the farm up and running, then the kids can take over and I'll move on. Maybe head out to Saguaro Valley? My brother would probably sell me a parcel of land. Build a house, settle in, and think of my next venture.* He knew it was his broken heart talking, but somehow, the thought of running away felt pretty good right then.

CHAPTER 28

ook fair season in full swing, Lucy, Lolly, and Wolfie were out in
the schools every day. Merlin's Closet ran book fairs for schools
in five towns, including the elementary and middle schools in
Horseshoe Crab Cove and the regional high school in Somers. They
ordered the books, had them shipped to the schools, then spent long
days setting up, selling, and breaking down displays. In addition to
Wolfie, they hired several locals, including Lynn, who had
volunteered to help when they needed her.

On a cold Monday morning, Lucy and Lynn walked into Barney,
the village elementary, together. "Are you sure you should be working
today?" Lucy asked. "The big day's Saturday."

"Mavis has everything under control. Besides, I'm glad of the
distraction. Otherwise, I'd just sit at home fretting. This'll be my last
day where I really feel free till it's all over. I'm going down to Groton
tomorrow, then people start coming in for the wedding."

"I'm looking forward to meeting your and Gus's families."

"And they you."

"Anyone need rides from the airport?"

"I think we're all set, thanks," Lynn said, pausing just inside the
door. As Lucy signed them in, she leaned against the wall, hand on
the side of her stomach.

When Lucy gazed up, she found Lynn grimacing, the pain evident in her eyes. "Lynn, what is it? Here, come sit." She led her to a chair by the school office door.

"It's too early," Lynn gasped. "She's not due for three weeks."

"How long have the contractions been going on?"

"Since breakfast."

"Lots of women have Braxton-Hicks for weeks before delivery. I know I did. Did your doctor tell you about them?"

Lynn nodded, her breathing coming in short gasps.

"Hang on," Lucy said. "I'm going to see if the school nurse is in."

Three minutes later, a tall, slender young man in a lab coat covered with children's drawings appeared. He smiled warmly, pushing his sandy hair from his forehead. "I'm Garrett White. Would you like to come back to my office?"

They helped Lynn to stand, and Lucy said, "You go. I'll be right in. I just want to make a quick call."

When she rejoined the others, she found Lynn sitting on a small examining table, Nurse White taking her blood pressure. "How is she?"

"Blood pressure's high. Everything else looks fine, but I haven't cared for pregnant women since my training. It would be my recommendation that you take her either to her doctor's office or to the hospital."

"No! Lucy's running today's book fair. She can't leave!"

"Yes, I can and I will. Wolfie's on his way, and Weezie's coming to help him. Why don't we call your doctor? Shall I call Gus too?"

Lynn gave her a wan smile. "Let's wait to see what the doctor says. I hate to pull him from work today. They've got so much going on."

Lucy nodded, a wave of sadness overcoming her as Lynn pulled her cell phone from her pocket. She had really loved hearing about the farms when she and Richard had been together. Even if they didn't see each other, they would phone in the evening to share their days. Now she had no idea what was happening out there.

After a quick conversation, Lynn clicked off. "The office is so close, they suggested that I come there."

"Okay. Thanks, Garrett."

"My pleasure. Good luck, Ms. Manguilli."

Midwife Cora Joulet set the heart monitor back on its hook and handed Lynn a tissue to wipe the gel from her belly. "Looks like you're in early stages of labor."

"Not Braxton-Hicks?"

"Nope, this is labor, but early. You've just begun to dilate. Is Gus on his way?"

"Not yet. I wanted to wait to call him till we knew."

"I'd give him a call now."

"But it's too early!"

"The baby's a good size."

Lynn grasped Cora's sleeve. "I'm not ready! I'm... We're getting married next week!"

"You're going to do fine. It's Monday. With rest, you'll be recovered in plenty of time."

"No, no, I can't! Lucy, tell her! I can't. It's too soon!"

Lucy held her hand. "You're going to do great, sweetie. Why don't I call Gus?"

Lynn nodded as another contraction began, and her face contorted with pain.

She found Gus's number on Lynn's phone. After several rings, she heard, "Hello, this is Gus Casey's phone, but he's unable to answer right now."

"Richard?"

"Lucy?"

"Yes, I need to speak to Gus." Her heart ached at the sound of his voice. The voice she loved so much.

"One of the mustangs is in distress, trying to break out of the enclosure. Gus is with him, trying to calm him down."

Oh Lord, that's all we need—expectant father trampled by a wild horse! "Well, get him out of there now! Lynn's in labor, and she needs him."

"Oh, of course. Right away."

"We're headed to Saint Elizabeth's in Bay Point. He can meet us there."

They clicked off, and she waited until Lynn's face relaxed and the contraction had passed. "Is it safe for me to drive her?"

"Yes, you have plenty of time. I'll be right behind you."

By the time they reached the hospital, Lynn was screaming in pain. As they pulled in, so did Gus's truck. Lucy breathed a huge sigh of relief.

He shut off the engine and raced to meet them. "How is she?"

"Cora says she's in early labor, but it's starting to get rough. Give me your keys. You two go in, and I'll deal with the cars. I'll find you. Go!"

CAR AND TRUCK PARKED, LUCY WAS HURRYING INTO THE HOSPITAL WHEN Richard called, "Lucy!"

She turned to spy Richard and Gail. Glad that Gail had accompanied him, she stopped and waited for them.

"How is she?" Gail asked.

"Gus took her in. They say it's early labor, but it's been pretty intense."

"How are you?" Richard asked, his beautiful eyes full of concern.

Her heart dropped, and every inch of her ached for him, ached for his strong arms around her, telling her everything would be all right. She took a deep breath. *Not now, Lucy!*

"I'm fine, thanks. Let's head in."

When they reached the labor floor, they were directed to the lounge, its peach-colored walls and muted pastel furnishings comforting. Someone wise and talented had decorated this space, Lucy thought as she sat down, the others beside her. No one spoke for several minutes until Lucy asked, "Did you manage to calm the horse?"

"Kyle was there. He gave him a mild sedative. Seemed to work."

"Poor thing," Lucy said absently.

"He's better off at the farm than starving in the wild," Gail said quietly.

"Of course," Lucy said. "That was a thoughtless remark. I'm sorry."

Gail stood. "Why don't I get us coffee or something? I'll find the cafeteria and grab a few things."

No sooner had Gail left than Gus appeared.

They both stood. "How is she?" Lucy said.

"Doing fine. Still early, they say. Listen, I have a huge favor to ask. The kids. I just called the school. Classes aren't over for two hours, and they'll keep them for a while, but—"

"Of course," Lucy said. "No worries. I'll go and collect them. They can stay with us as long as you need. Amy'll be delighted."

"Are you sure? I was going to ask about sitters," Gus said, one eye on the door.

"I've got this, Gus. You go back to Lynn. Can you just call the school and let them know I have your permission to collect them?"

Gus stepped forward and hugged her. "Thank you so much!"

As he disappeared, they both sat down.

"I'll go with you," he said. "Gail can take the car back."

"That's not necessary."

"I want to."

Lucy met his eyes and saw the fiery determination. The same determination that had made him a very wealthy man. "Okay," she said quietly. "I was thinking I might stop at the book fair before I pick up the kids to see how Weezie and Wolfie are doing."

"I'm happy to go with you."

"Okay, let's wait till Gail gets back."

They sat side by side, neither knowing quite what to say. Finally, she broke the silence. "I hear things are going well at the farm."

"Yup. Things are buzzing. In fact, I've been feeling somewhat superfluous lately. Between the kids and Gus and his crew, I'm not really needed. I've been putting my energy into the vineyard startup, but as soon as I can pull Wolfie in, I'll probably step back from that too."

Lucy wondered at the subtext of his words, but didn't inquire. It almost sounded as if he were getting ready to move on. *Of course, that's what Richard Morgan does. Starts companies, makes lots of money, then moves on.*

Both of them stared straight ahead, which was how Gail found them several minutes later. She took a read of the room, then set cups of coffee and tea on the table in front of them. "There are bagels and cream cheese in the bag. Fruit too. Any word?"

Lucy shook herself. "Thanks. Gus came in briefly, but he said it's still early. I'm...we're going to head out pretty soon to pick up Dulcie and Cal from day care."

"Oh, that's right. Can I help?"

"I think I'm set. They can come back to my house. I have Amy to help. Of course, you're welcome to come over."

"I'm going with Lucy," he declared, standing up.

Gail gave him a puzzled look, then turned to her. "What should I do? Do you think I should go? I mean, I'm not family or anything. I mostly came 'cause Dad wanted to."

Lucy sighed. *What a jumbled mess things are. The man I adore is beside me and we're barely speaking, even though he's run to my aid.* Smiling at Gail, she said, "Lynn's labor could go on all day or longer. It's probably best if we all take off. I'll take one of these coffees to go."

"Maybe I'll leave the food at the nurse's station," Gail said, stuffing everything back into the bag. "Unless one of you is hungry?"

Both declined as they grabbed jackets and bags. They walked out together, and when they reached the lot, Lucy turned to him. "Are you sure you want to come along? You must have things to do at home."

He grinned, and she thought he'd never looked handsomer, even with a day-old beard and rumpled hair. "Didn't I just tell you I'm superfluous out there?"

Lucy smiled. "Yes, you did, but I don't believe you."

Hands on hips, Gail observed their repartee. "So...does anyone need a ride from me or what?"

Richard hugged her. "You go ahead, sweetheart. I'll Uber home later."

"Okay, then. Bye!" She waved over her shoulder, headed for her father's Land Rover.

~

"How'd this happen?" Lolly whispered, taking her aside as father and son chatted. They were in the Barney School gymnasium, the book fair in full swing. Children and their teachers milled about, picking up books, reading back covers, skimming. Weezie was manning the cash drawer.

"Met at the hospital, and he insisted on coming to help with Dulcie and Cal. What are you doing here? Aren't you supposed to be at the high school?"

"All set up, but kids don't shop till two, so I came to check on these two. They're doing great, by the way. We should hire Weezie."

"We can't afford her."

"So?" Lolly said.

"So nothing. We've barely spoken."

"How does that feel?"

"Awful. I can hardly breathe around him."

"Must be love."

"Stop it!" Lucy jabbed her just as Richard looked their way and smiled.

"We've got this covered, partner. Why don't you and Mr. Bedroom Eyes take off and have lunch before you start your babysitting marathon?"

"You sure?"

"Absolutely!"

~

"It's very good to see you," Richard said as they sat in the Crab Café. Milly had taken their orders and brought hot tea to both of them.

"You too," Lucy said. "Richard, I'm so sorry for how things have turned out. For hurting you and for causing our estrangement." She ached to feel his arms around her, suffusing her with warmth and love.

"I'm sorry if I led you on."

"No need to be sorry. I rushed things, and in the process destroyed the most meaningful, important relationship I've had in over twenty years."

"So here we are. Friends?"

"Of course." He reached across the table and patted her hand. "I'm thinking of going away."

"Oh?" Her heart constricted, and for a second, Lucy felt faint.

"As I said, the farm's running well and I'm really not needed. That's one of the perks of having lots of smart kids and hiring good people. I'm thinking I'll head out west. See my brother, then head for California wine country. Maybe after that I'll go to France for a while. Not sure yet."

"Sounds like a long trip."

He gave her a tired smile. "Could be. I make plans as I go along. It's worked for thirty years."

"What happened to putting down roots?"

"I guess I'm not suited for that kind of thing. Longest we were anywhere was Maine, but even that didn't last. I may spend some time up there and on Long Island touring vineyards before I head west."

"Here you go, folks," Milly said, placing salads in front of each. "Can I get you anything else?"

"All set," Lucy said, smiling at her. She couldn't look at Richard for fear of crying, so she gazed down at her spinach salad, feeling slightly nauseous. After ten minutes of picking at it, she looked up. "Would you mind if we get going? I'm not very hungry, and it's almost time to pick up the kids." She noticed that his plate was clean, no trace of his salad remaining.

"Of course." He waved to Milly and asked for the check.

As she drove the short distance to the nursery school, Lucy struggled to maintain control. *Don't cry, don't break down. This is your doing. You drove him away just like you did Rob! There, I've said it. I'm unlovable. Always have been, always will be.*

They spent the afternoon entertaining Dulcie and Cal. Dulcie continually asked if they'd heard from the hospital, but Cal was oblivious. He loved Rob, and they were playing football in the family room with a soft stuffed ball.

"Your son's great with kids," Richard said. "Amy too."

"Yes. They've both worked at summer camps. In fact, after seeing Emma's Dream when we were in Saguaro, I'd love for them to be counselors out there. I've been meaning to call Maggie Morgan and inquire."

"Great experience."

"Hard to leave their friends all summer. That's the only catch."

He nodded. "Listen, I'm feeling superfluous here as well, so I'm going to take off unless I can help in any way? Get takeout for dinner, perhaps?"

"No, we're fine. The kids want pizza. We'll have it delivered."

"Well, let me phone for a ride. Excuse me."

As he turned to step out of the room, she said, "That's silly. Either Rob or I can take you."

"Not on your life. He's in the middle of an epic contest."

"Well, I'm not. Put that away, I can run you home."

"No way," he said, touching her arm. "I've got Uber on speed dial. See?" He held the phone to his ear. "Yup, it's Richard Morgan. Somers? Ten minutes. Terrific." He rattled off Lucy's address and clicked off. "Now let's go see how the game's progressing."

And that was it. End of story. He left ten minutes later, Lucy confused and heartbroken.

RICHARD WAS WELL ACQUAINTED WITH MONTY, THE UBER DRIVER WHO drove a lime-green van. In between small talk, he thought about the tumultuous day. *I was right to keep my distance and not try to resume things. She's still like a deer in the headlights, and I don't want to cause further distress.* The thought of leaving Horseshoe Crab Cove and Lucy was agonizing, but he sensed it was the right thing. It was painful every time he heard her name.

Then there was Gail's strange about-face. That was about to drive him crazy. Every other minute, his prickly daughter was bringing up Lucy's name, asking when he was going to see her, wondering when she was coming to dinner. When he asked why she cared, Gail stated that she'd been wrong and that she liked Lucy and thought they'd be great together. *When did life get so topsy-turvy?*

CHAPTER 29

"Sorcha Elizabeth Casey is so beautiful," Lucy said, gazing down at the rosy-cheeked infant in Lynn's arms.

Lynn beamed. "She is, isn't she?"

"And she came quick, huh?"

"I'll say. No sooner did Cora say we were in for a long day than things heated up fast."

"Was it okay with just you and Gus?"

"Perfect. He was wonderful. Poor guy's exhausted, and now he has to get the kids to bed."

"I wish you'd have let me keep them. I was surprised the hospital discharged you."

"I wanted to come home, and Gus didn't want the kids to meet Sorcha in the hospital. I feel so much better here, in my own bed, even if it is a rental house and a rental bed."

"Well, you've got enough food for a month. Your fridge and freezer are well stocked."

"Please thank everyone for us."

"Now what about the next few days? Have you got help?"

"Gus is taking the rest of the week and most of next week off. He was planning to do it in March when the baby was due, but this is better. Dennis and the rest of them can manage."

"Good. Best to have Daddy around so you can all bond. How are you feeling?"

"I'm tired, but otherwise, I feel great. The kids'll go to school the rest of the week so I can take lots of naps in preparation for the wedding."

"Are you sure about this?"

"Yes! Gus and I discussed it, and we don't want to postpone. I'll be fine. I can sit Friday night and Saturday too, except for the ceremony."

"Well, I'm happy to help with last-minute things."

"Thanks. Gus's sister Laurie and his parents arrive tomorrow, and they'll have a rental car, so they can pitch in. The Caseys are staying through next week to help."

"And your honeymoon?"

Lynn smiled, giving Lucy a wistful look. "We decided to cancel. Much as I wanted to get away to the warmth of the Caribbean, we'd have had to take Sorcha and leave the others, and we decided the timing wasn't right. We got a full refund on the airfare and credit at the resort. We'll go next year, just the two of us, after the baby's weaned, or maybe all five of us."

"You've been busy," Lucy said.

"Honestly, it's a bit overwhelming, but I'm trying to take care of things systematically. Thank God for you and Mavis and everyone," Lynn said.

"Can I bring you anything?" Lucy asked.

"No, I'm good. Gus takes good care of us all."

"Well, please don't hesitate to phone or text if you need something."

"Thank you. As you can imagine, Richard has offered everything but the moon in the way of helping. He's such a kind man and incredibly generous, just like his brother."

"Yes, he is," Lucy said. "Hope you get a good night's sleep. Is she beginning to feed?"

"Took to the breast immediately. I feel so lucky."

"Night," Lucy said, slipping out. She could hear Gus's spirited reading of what sounded like a Dr. Seuss book. *What a good dad he is.* She thought back to Rob reading to their kids, using many wonderful, funny voices.

∼

"HOW'S TORNADO DOING?" RICHARD ASKED WEEZIE AS THEIR MONDAY meeting commenced in the farmhouse dining room. He referred to the mustang they'd had to sedate the previous Friday.

"Better, calmer," she said. "Hasn't needed another tranquilizer. That's progress. Not sure how he'll be with Gus gone for so long."

"I can't believe they're actually going through with the wedding," Gail said.

Weezie waved her hand. "Women all over the world give birth and are back working in the fields the next day."

"Well, I hope we won't see that!" her father said. "Rich, what's new?"

Rich gave an update on the status of several Morgan Enterprises businesses, then went on to tell them about progress on the various building projects underway at Morgan's Fire. Finally, he pulled out his notes on the vineyard.

"Zeke and his assistant are ready to come whenever we say the word. I'm thinking in another week or two, his cottage'll be livable. The assistant can move in any time. The bunkhouse is ready. She'll have one of the end units. Those are bigger, with a sitting room and private bathroom. All the units are pretty incredible, if I do say so myself."

"Should be since they were designed by my nephew, one of the country's finest up-and-coming architects." Sam Morgan had designed the bunkhouses and most of the new construction as well as the renovations. Based in Baltimore, Sam had already made a name for himself as an innovative designer of zero-energy homes and commercial spaces.

"Wish he and Rose would move to New England," Weezie said. "I like them."

"Not with her job. It's major," Gail said.

"Anything else?" Richard said.

"I'm heading into town," Rich said, gathering his things.

"Bye, son." Richard watched his oldest, thinking how proud he was of him. *He's ready. He's already in charge of most things.*

"So, Dad, how are things with Lucy?" Weezie asked, exchanging a look with her sister.

"Fine."

"So...?" Weezie said.

"Let's leave it there," he said.

Gail shook her head at her sister.

Weezie rolled her eyes. "Well, do what you want, but she's a great person, and I know you love her and she loves you."

Abruptly, Richard stood, his chair scraping across the floor. "Apparently, that's not enough. I'm going down to the barn."

"Right behind you!" Weezie called.

As Richard slammed the back door, Gail turned to her. "Leave him alone. You're only making it worse. You know he's thinking of leaving."

"What?"

"I found notes in the office about flights, and Uncle Ben left a message the other night saying they'd love to have him. He's preparing to bolt just like he's done since Mom died."

"But why?"

"Because he's heartbroken about Lucy and can't stand to be in the same town as she is. Easier to run away than face her."

"Well, that's just dumb."

"What's dumb is you pestering him about it. Let him stew, and maybe, just maybe, he'll find a reason to stay. I'm hoping that Wolfie comes through and decides to run the vineyard. That would give Dad a boost."

"Let's talk to little brother, then. Make him understand how important it is."

"You're talking about Dad's clone," Gail said. "You push Wolfie and he'll bolt, just like Dad."

"Geez," Weezie said, sipping cold coffee.

"Geez indeed," Gail said, gazing out the window, spying her father talking to Dennis Farrell.

CHAPTER 30

"I don't know how I'm going to get through tonight and tomorrow," Lucy said, sitting opposite Elise Nolan. She'd called the previous evening, and the therapist had agreed to an emergency session at 7:30 in the morning.

"What's concerning you?" Elise asked as she quietly sipped her tea.

"It's so awkward, and, if I'm being honest, painful."

"Because?"

"Because we had something really incredible, and it's gone."

"Are you sure?"

"He told me he's thinking of leaving Horseshoe Crab Cove."

Elise's coal-black eyes registered surprise. "Oh? What about his new business venture here? The farm and all?"

"He claims his kids and employees have everything under control."

"Hmm... I had the impression that he was passionate about the farm."

"Me too."

"Could it be that he's leaving for the same reason you're worried about this weekend? Too painful to see you?"

"Maybe, but that's not the way he explained things."

"Self-preservation maybe?"

"I guess I don't know him as well as I thought I did."

"In what way?"

"Well, if he can just up and leave when the going gets rough, is that the kind of partner I want?"

Elise suppressed a smile. "He did propose."

"Yes, and then he disappeared."

"After you rejected him."

"I did not reject him! I asked for some time and space."

"Which he seems to have given you."

Lucy stared at the therapist. *Whose side is she on? Isn't she meant to support me?* "I'm feeling uncomfortable with this conversation right now."

"Is there something that would help?"

You taking my side for one! "I'm not sure. I guess I'll go back to my concerns about getting through the next two days."

"There are a couple of things I can suggest. Carefully plan where you will position yourself. Do you know who you'll sit with tonight?"

"No, but I suspect they'll put me with Kyle and Harriet. I know it won't be at Richard's table."

"What about tomorrow? For the ceremony? Reception?"

"Same. I'll be with family. Amy and Rob were invited to the wedding, so I'll be with them."

"Good. You can also ask your sister or one of your friends to check in with you from time to time during the open, mingling times."

Suddenly, Lucy's eyes filled with tears. "I miss him."

"Yes."

"Is that crazy?"

"Not from where I'm sitting."

"What does that mean?"

Elise paused, setting her mug down, rearranging her legs. She appeared to be considering how to answer. "I'm going go out on a limb here and say that from what I know about you, you are deeply in love with Richard. It would be natural for you to miss him."

"I don't know how to go back...to fix things."

"Is it about fixing things or moving forward?"

"Both, I guess."

"Perhaps you could speak to him at some point and say you'd like to see him...to talk things through?"

"What good would it do at this point?"

"I think it might surprise you and him. A good honest, open discussion where you both express your feelings as well as your needs and wants."

Lucy wiped her eyes. "I don't have high hopes, but I'll think about it."

They talked a while longer, then her time was up. She was meeting Gus and Lynn's sisters at the American Legion Hall to decorate for the rehearsal dinner. As she headed back up the street, she realized that her heart felt lighter. She had no idea what the next few days would bring, but there was something about admitting her feelings and how much she missed Richard that had been freeing.

Deep in thought, she practically crashed into Rob, emerging from the Crab Café with several bags. "Hey, Luce... Lucy," he said, smiling.

At that moment, she wanted to slap him for using the familiar nickname again. Instead, she said, "Hello," stepping out of the way to let him pass.

"How're things?"

"Fine. I'm in kind of a hurry."

"I'd love to have lunch sometime."

Suddenly, all the anger and pain flashed in front of her eyes. *How dare he?* "Well, I wouldn't. Rob, this is the last time I will ask you not to make overtures to me."

"It's just a friendly overture."

"Well, I can't be your friend right now. Someday, maybe, and of course when we're discussing the kids, but beyond that, I don't feel friendship with you, only betrayal."

"I'm sorry. I'll never forgive myself."

"Well, you should. I forgave you, I just don't want to hang out with you."

"Fine, I get it. Better get these back to the hungry hordes. If they don't get their coffee and bagels, it's not pretty. Have fun at the big wedding."

"Not so big, but thanks."

"If Mavis is in charge, it's big. See you."

There was something slightly creepy about how he always seemed to know her business. She wondered if he pumped the kids for information or had other sources. *Enough about him*, she thought, heading up the stairs to Merlin's Closet.

CHAPTER 31

"T his is perfect," Barb Manguilli said as she stood with Lucy surveying the American Legion Hall. Along with Laurie Casey, Gus's sister, who had just departed, the three had spent the morning decorating the plain interior with its white beadboard walls and aged hardwood floors. Long tables were covered with brightly patterned tablecloths, and vases of flowers lined the centers. They had hung streamers and balloons from the ceiling and walls, and the bar and serving tables were set up and ready.

"Yes, we did good," Lucy said, arm around Barb's shoulders. *Mavis would have a coronary if she saw it, but she can be as fancy as she wants tomorrow.*

"This is so Lynn and Gus!"

"I'm glad. I'm sure the food'll be great too. Salters does a terrific job."

"My mom's not a fan of barbecue," Barb said. "Not that she's eating much now. But they're making salmon for her."

Lucy felt a pang of sadness for Barb and her family. She had met Sorcha Manguilli the day before. Their beautiful, impossibly thin mother had put on a brave face, but she was clearly in pain. "I'm so glad she's here."

"She is too. Our dad's been great. Since she got sick, he's been by her side, like they never got divorced. Lynn's probably told you about their weird living arrangements?"

"A little."

"Since the divorce, Mom's lived in the house and Dad in the carriage house. The day after her diagnosis, he moved back in. She protested for about thirty seconds, but I think it's been good for her. For both of them."

"There's no right way to do divorce," Lucy said. "No rule book. You do the best you can and hope it's right for you."

"Your ex lives in town, I understand."

"Yes, he does."

"How's that?"

"Good for the kids. Has had its ups and downs for me, but I'm dealing. What do you say we head out?"

"Ooh, look at the time. A bunch of us are meeting for lunch at the Café. Want to come?"

"Thanks, but I'm going to head to the office for a few hours."

They strolled around the corner and up Main Street. The Crab Café was a short walk, and they said goodbye at the door, Lucy waving to the family seated inside. She caught a glimpse of Richard and breathed a sigh of relief that she'd declined Barb's invitation.

"See you tonight," she said, hugging her companion.

"Didn't expect to see you," Lolly said as she stepped into the office.

Lucy nodded at Wolfie as she headed for her desk. "Looks great in here."

"Thank our assistant extraordinaire. How'd the decorating go?" Lolly asked.

"The Legion Hall never looked so good," Lucy said, although the sadness of seeing Richard still lingered.

"What's wrong?" asked her partner, who always read her like a book.

Lucy shook her head, looking over at Wolfie, who was busy packing books. "Nothing."

"Okay, out with it."

"I don't want to talk about it."

Wolfie stood up. "Should I make myself scarce for a few minutes?"

"Absolutely not!" Lucy snapped.

Lolly made a face and gestured for him to sit down. He looked as if he'd happily jump out the window if he could.

Lucy buried herself in paperwork, and the others left her alone.

CHAPTER 32

"Wow, Mom, you look awesome," Rob said as Lucy came into the kitchen.

"I'll say," Amy echoed.

Lucy smiled. She was used to Amy's compliments, but her son rarely noticed what she wore or how she looked. At Lolly's insistence, they'd driven to Northport the previous Wednesday to shop at Margaret's, a boutique dress shop.

Margaret, the owner, was a forty-something whirlwind who looked twenty and moved like it. Her expert eyes sized one up, and everything she brought to the dressing room was flattering, gorgeous, and costly. Lucy had bought a little black dress and a peach off-the-shoulder dress for the wedding. She had also bought the jeans she now wore, the most expensive pair she would ever own, and the casual gray marled cotton top that hugged her figure, revealing just a hint of cleavage.

"Thank you both," she said, bowing slightly.

"Pretty fancy for a barbecue at the Legion hall," he said.

Lucy's face dropped. "You think so? Too much?"

"No!" Amy said, giving her brother a sharp look. "You look perfect, Mom!"

"I'm not sure I'll be able to eat, much less sit comfortably in these jeans, but they do stretch."

"Can we shop at Margaret's for me sometime?" Amy said.

"We'll see. Dinner's in the fridge, and I shouldn't be too late. What are you guys doing tonight, anyway?"

"I'm staying home, and Celia's coming over," her daughter said.

"I'm going to Andy's," Rob said.

Lucy grabbed a jacket and her purse. "Well, have fun. Rob, is your suit pressed for tomorrow?"

He gave her a look. "Yes, Mom."

"Great. Kyle and Harriet just pulled in. See you!"

When they arrived, it appeared that most people were there. Lynn's family and the Caseys greeted people at the door, and a crowd milled about the bar and appetizer tables. The caterer had set out guacamole, salsas, cheese platters, and vegetables. They were now passing chicken skewers and a variety of hot appetizers.

"Can I get you ladies a drink?" Kyle asked.

They both requested white wine, and he headed for the bar, where a group of farm workers were congregated. As the sisters surveyed the crowd, Polly Larrabee found them. "Hi, Harriet! Lucy! So good to see you."

They both hugged Lynn's slender former colleague.

"How's life out west?" Harriet said.

"Busy. The Cottage has been hopping. Lynn's replacement, Jo Gaines, is settling in, and I'm juggling things with baby Perry."

"I met Jo briefly when we were out for Christmas. How's that working out?" Harriet asked.

"She's not Lynn, and I miss my friend terribly, but Jo's terrific, and the kids love her."

"Where's baby Perry tonight?" Lucy asked. "I dying to see her and Jasper too, of course."

"With a sitter. We knew it would be too much with Jasper and the baby. Our son is still quite the hellion. We brought Daisy with us. Do you remember her? Daisy Springer, who works at the Cottage? Spark and Ben Morgan paid her way and hired substitutes for the two of us for this week."

Harriet chuckled. "Of course they did. How are the gray foxes anyway?"

"Great. Having fun with Valley Stables, looking forward to your wedding."

"Us too," Lucy said. "I can't wait to get back to that beautiful valley. And our sisters are really excited to see it after hearing so much from us."

"Is your mom here tonight?" Polly asked.

"No, but she'll be at the wedding tomorrow," Lucy said.

"Will be wonderful to see her. I love your mom."

Kyle returned with their wines, and Kevin Larrabee, Polly's husband, joined them and handed her a beer.

"Hey, great to see everyone," Kevin said. "Weezie Morgan gave us a tour today. This is a beautiful area."

Harriet smiled as Kyle's arm circled her shoulders. "That it is."

"And here comes the Morgan entourage," Kyle said. "Hey, Uncle Dick!" He waved, gesturing for Richard, Gail, Rich, and Weezie to join them.

Lucy's heart stopped, and she struggled to take a breath. She took a gulp of wine and stepped back as the group approached. Her retreat did not go unnoticed by her sister. Harriet touched her arm, then laced her fingers through hers.

Dressed casually in jeans, blue sport shirt, and gray sweater, Richard look gorgeous as ever. He hugged Polly and shook Kevin's hand, then greeted the others. His eyes found hers, and he nodded. Gail then took the lead and herded her family forward as Rich and his father headed for the bar.

"Another younger silver fox," Polly whispered, watching the men. "We thought you two might be starting something when you visited last year," she said to Lucy.

Silver fox, indeed. "Yes we've dated a bit. Would you all excuse me? I need to use the ladies' room." Lucy hurried across the room and into the bathroom. As she closed the door, she let out her breath. *I wonder if I can hide in here all night?*

When she finally emerged, Gail Morgan stood near the door. "I've been waiting for you."

"Oh? What's up?"

"This has got to stop."

"Not now, Gail."

"Then when? My father's a basket case, and you're like a scared rabbit every time you catch a glimpse of him."

"I don't know when, but tonight is definitely not the time. You look pretty, by the way."

Lucy wondered if the extra effort her companion made with her clothes and makeup might have something to do with Tim Miller, who was working part-time for the Salters and was here tonight overseeing the roasting pit and barbecue grills set up behind the hall.

"Thanks," Gail said, blushing slightly as her eyes scanned the room.

"I saw Tim a few minutes ago. He's out back, but he'll be in when they serve."

Gail gave her a look, then smiled. "That obvious, huh?"

"He's a great guy."

"I thought I might catch him to talk furniture. We'd like to get one or a couple of his pieces for Lynn and Gus."

"Great idea."

"Here are two of the prettiest ladies in the room."

As Richard appeared from behind them, Lucy jumped. "Oh, hello."

"Might I have a word?" he asked, ignoring Gail and gazing at Lucy.

Gail grinned. "I'm going to see a man about a coffee table."

"Richard, I'm not sure this is the time or place."

"Well, I am." Gently, he took hold of her elbow. "Won't take a minute."

He steered them toward the rear of the hall out the side door to a storage room filled with old furniture, shelves of dishes and cleaning supplies, and various machines and barrels.

"Richard, this is ridiculous."

He closed the door behind them. "I don't think so. Now, please hear me out. I've been a horse's ass since New Year's Eve, and I want to apologize. Just because you don't want to marry me doesn't mean that you and I can't see each other and have a close, loving relationship. My kids are right—I don't like the 'no' word, but in this case, I'm just going to have to swallow my arrogant pride and accept it. I can't eat, I can't sleep, and I've been turning myself in knots planning trips, new businesses, and anything to distract myself, but the truth is I miss you. And if I go to Arizona, Napa Valley, France, or who knows where, I'll *still* miss you."

"Richard, I—"

"No. Please don't say anything, Lucy. Not now. I wanted to get that off my chest so that you can think about whether you even *want* to see me anymore as a friend or whatever. Now, come on, let's get you out of this grungy hole and back to the party."

"But I—"

"Not tonight. Tonight is Gus and Lynn's night. Would you take a walk with me in the morning? I could come by any time that's convenient."

She nodded.

"Would nine work?"

"Yes," she said softly. "Why don't I come to the farm? Haven't been out there in a while."

"Perfect." Without another word, he propelled her back into the hall, where people were taking their seats for the first course. As he and Lucy parted, he squeezed her hand then let her go, Lucy to sit with Kyle and Harriet, Richard with his family.

"Where'd you disappear to?" Harriet asked, studying her face. "You're all red. Are you overheated?"

"No, fine," Lucy said, waving her hand. But was she? If he'd let her get a word in edgewise, what would she have said? *I love you and miss you every second of every day with every fiber of my being? I'm scared. I'm still not ready?*

CHAPTER 33

"Morning," Lucy said as Richard opened the farmhouse door, a grin creasing his chiseled face. *Looks like a kid in a candy store*, she thought, returning his smile. *He also looks good enough to eat!*

"How about we walk out to the corrals," he said. "The men have just put the horses out. We can take a peek and then head out along the path through the east meadow. Might be a bit muddy now that the snow's gone, but it should be okay."

"Sounds good," she said as he grabbed his jacket from a peg rack in the mudroom. They had ridden along the east path several times. It led to the cliffs overlooking the river, and if you turned south, it eventually met the eighteen-mile trail that circled the peninsula and Horseshoe Crab Cove.

"I'm so glad to see you," he said as they strolled toward the barn.

The wind had whipped up, and it was cool and breezy. Lucy wished she'd worn another layer. She raised the collar on her jacket. "Me too, you."

"You cold?"

"Just a little."

"Well, we can't have that. Come on, let's go back. We have plenty of stuff at the house."

"That's okay," she said. "My car's right here. I have a fleece in the back." He waited while she shed her leather jacket, then shrugged into a black fleece. Once she was zipped up in her jacket, she rummaged around until she uncovered mittens and a knitted hat. Now bundled up, she faced him, grinning. "Warmth over stylishness."

"You look extremely stylish. Farm chic. And that cap brings out the lovely flecks of blue in your eyes."

"You always know the right thing to say, don't you?"

"I try. Ready?"

As they strolled around the barn and corrals, he chattered happily, describing all the latest building projects, the progress with the mustangs, and the plans for the winery. It was clear that he took delight from all these ventures, and his enthusiasm was infectious. After touring the barn and corrals and meeting all the horses, he said, "You warm enough?"

"Perfect."

"Shall we walk a ways?"

Lucy linked her arm through his, and they set off. "If I forget to tell you later, I'm having a really good time and am so glad to be here."

He squeezed her gloved hand. "Thank you for saying that."

"You must be cold," she said.

"Not a hardy Mainer like me. I have gloves in my pocket if I need 'em."

They walked in silence as the path led through the meadow and up a small rise. At the top, it followed the crest of the hill for several miles in each direction. The river trail was straight ahead, but he turned north and led her a short way to where a bench sat.

"This is new," she said. "It's lovely."

"Pam brought it when she came at Christmas. Took us a while to figure out where we wanted to put it. We settled on this spot because Laura loved open fields and wildflowers."

Lucy gazed down at the ornately carved bench, teak flowers and leaves trailing over its back and down its strong, sturdy legs. A small brass plaque on the front edge of the seat was nestled between a cluster of vines and read: *Laura Morgan, beloved wife and mother: "Cross the meadow and the stream and listen as the peaceful water brings peace upon your soul."*

"Can't hear the water from here unless it's stormy, but she would have liked this place. Besides, we didn't want to leave her in Maine all by herself now that Pam's moving down."

"So Pam's definitely moving?"

"Yes, in a month or two."

"How nice for you."

"Yes. Want to sit?"

In answer, she sat, and he beside her. For several minutes, they gazed out at the fields that stretched as far west as the eye could see. "This is such an amazing property. So much open space," Lucy said.

"And it will stay that way forever if I have anything to say about it. I'm in the process of turning a large chunk of it over to the Nature Conservancy."

Of course you are, she thought. *I love this kind, generous man with all my heart. What are the right words to tell him that while I also take care of my own fragile self?* She turned to peer into his beautiful dark eyes.

"Richard, I meant what I said before. I'm so glad to see you. I've missed you terribly, but I couldn't think how to fix things. I wanted to give you space. Maybe I was wrong. I'm still struggling to figure things out, but I do know that I love you."

"I'm glad," he said, taking her hand. "Friends?"

"Friends."

"Okay if I call you to do things? Dinners? Lunches? Breakfasts? Walks?"

"Of course." She rested her head against his shoulder.

He grinned. "In my mind, I'm throwing my arms around you, making wild, passionate love to you."

She smiled, patting his knee. "These kinds of thoughts have crossed my mind too. I've certainly missed that."

"One step at a time?"

"Yes." She glanced down at her watch. "Oh, look at the time. I need to get back. I promised to get to the church early and check the flowers and all."

"Isn't that LaSalle woman handling that?"

She smiled. "Mavis is handling the reception, but she's not involved with the ceremony. Lynn and Gus wanted to organize it themselves. The two sisters are doing the flowers. I helped order them along with vases and stuff. I need to pick them up at eleven, then meet Laurie and Barb."

"They're lucky to have you in their lives, Gus and Lynn."

"We're lucky to have each other. Come on, we've gotta practice power walking!"

AS LUCY UNLOADED BOXES OF FLOWERS, VASES, RIBBONS, AND SUPPLIES at the tiny village chapel, she still felt the warmth of Richard's lips on her cheek, a friendly goodbye kiss at her car. She was still smiling when Laurie and Barb drove up.

After an hour, they had filled all the Mason jars with colorful wildflowers and wrapped flowers around the outside rails and on pew backs along the aisle. Sorcha Manguilli had insisted upon purchasing the altar arrangement, a profusion of color and greenery that trailed along and down both sides of the table at the front of the sanctuary. "It looks perfect," Barb declared, admiring their work before giving Laurie, then Lucy high fives.

Lucy nodded. "Yes, it does."

Tears in her eyes, Laurie gazed from one to the other. "Thank you for this and well...everything! People have been so incredibly nice to my family. Makes me want to move here immediately."

"We'd love that," Lucy said, patting her arm.

"You know, we never thought my brother would recover from losing Lissie. They'd been together their whole lives. Then Lynn came along, and the Gus we knew and loved returned to us. He's so happy, and so are the kids and all of us. Mom and Dad are literally over the moon."

"As are the Manguillis, I can tell you," Barb said. "And to have something joyful like this to think about has given Mom such a boost."

All three teary-eyed now, they hugged.

"Okay, now," Lucy said. "Who's ready for a wedding? Time to get back and get dressed!"

CHAPTER 34

Lucy smiled at her reflection in the full-length mirror. Her silk peach off-the-shoulder dress fit like a second skin, hugging every curve. She felt wanton and sexy the minute she slipped it over her head. "That dress was made for you!" Margaret had exclaimed as soon as she stepped out of the dressing room, and Lolly had concurred. The boutique owner had paired suede buff five-inch heels and pearl earrings and a necklace with it.

After one last brush through her hair, she grabbed a beige cashmere shawl and called, "Hey, guys, you ready?"

A few minutes later, she stood with her son in the family room as he straightened his tie. "You look very handsome."

"Thanks. You look incredible, Mom."

"Thank you. Where's your sister?"

"Primping."

"Am not," Amy said, twirling as she came into the room wearing a wide floral-print skirt and lacy off-white top.

"Oh, honey, you look fantastic!"

"Thanks, so do you."

"Let's go, then!"

$\sim$

"Oh my, Mavis has outdone herself as usual," Helen said as she walked arm in arm into the Netherfield Persimmon Room with Lucy and Harriet. Kyle had let them off and was parking the car.

"When does she not outdo herself?" Harriet said.

"So happy for Lynn and Gus," Lucy said, head resting on her mother's shoulder.

"You look beautiful, my dear," Helen said. "Both of you!"

Harriet chuckled. "My dress is pretty, and it got a whistle out of my fiancé, but it doesn't hold a candle to that. I wonder if Margaret ever has wedding dresses."

"We'll find you a perfect dress," Lucy said. "Never fear, plenty of time."

"Hello, hello!" Mavis called, rushing up to hug her dear friend and fellow Darn Yarner. "Looking lovely as always, Hellie." Mavis's dark hair was pulled back in a chignon with rhinestone clips that matched her necklace and earrings. She wore Dior, a deep purple sheath that deepened the color in her violet eyes.

"This is beautiful," Helen said, waving her arms wide. "How do you do it?"

"Practice. Lots of practice. How was the ceremony?"

"Beautiful," Harriet said.

Lucy nodded. "Full love and joyful tears."

"They're a lovely couple. Such a privilege to arrange this special day for them and their families. Her mother is so fragile, yet so courageous and beautiful."

"Yes," Lucy said as they watched Sorcha Manguilli make her way in on her husband's arm. "I do hope she beats the odds."

Her companions nodded.

Mavis waved her hands. "Okay, ladies, I must see to the seating. Mingle, mingle, mingle. Here comes that cute boyfriend of yours, Harriet. Golly, I wish my Lolly could find someone like him."

"That's one crazy broad," Kyle said, joining them. "What can I get my favorite ladies to drink?"

"Nothing for me, thanks," Lucy said. "I'm going to find Amy. I'll be back. Mum, are you okay?"

"Of course. Go."

As she searched for her daughter, Lucy also scanned the room for Richard. She'd caught his eye at the church, but they hadn't spoken. Finally, she spied Amy talking with Gail and Weezie. "I didn't know Amy rode," Weezie said as she approached. "We need her at the farm! What about a summer job?"

"That's up to her," Lucy said, arm circling Amy's waist.

"Gran and Mom have been trying to get me a job at the camp out west."

"Emma's Dream?" Weezie asked, wide-eyed. "Not fair. We need her here. Maybe we should start a camp here. God knows Dad's got enough property."

Gail gave Lucy a look as she rolled her eyes at her sister. "Dad says Uncle Ben told him that Emma's Dream was a labor of love for Maggie."

Lip out, hands on hips, Weezie said, "Doesn't mean we couldn't start one on Morgan's Fire."

"Uh-oh, what are you gals plotting now?" Richard winked at Lucy as he draped his arms around his daughters. "Start what at Morgan's Fire?"

"A camp like Emma's Dream," Weezie said. "I think it's a terrific idea, but as usual, Gail has thrown cold water all over it."

"Well, something to bring up at our weekly meeting. Have you talked to your brother about it?"

"No, and he's even less likely than her to think it's a good idea."

"Would you excuse me, Lucy, Amy?" Gail said. "I'm going to get a very large drink and circulate."

"Good idea!" he said.

Amy excused herself to join her friends, and Weezie spied Dennis Farrell and flew off, leaving them alone.

"Just you and me, babe."

"Looks like it."

"Want to get a drink?"

"Love to."

They strolled to the bar together. Lucy asked for champagne, and

Richard ordered a Tanqueray martini , extra dry with a twist. "Always have one martini at weddings."

"Oh?"

"Brings good luck to the bride and groom."

"I've never heard that."

"Where are you sitting?"

"Table six, with Mother and my sister."

"I'm with the farm crew. Think we could switch place cards so we can play friendly footsy under the table?"

She laughed, taking his arm. "Not if Mavis has anything to say about it."

"Well, then you promise to save me a dance or twenty?"

"Yes," she said, squeezing his arm as they strolled around the edge of the beautiful room.

"This is quite a place LaSalle's got here."

"Don't let her catch you calling her that."

"I know her ex-husband. Did I ever tell you that?"

"No."

"Yup. Invested in a couple of his plays. Didn't make out too badly either."

"Recently?"

"No. About twenty-five years ago. It was Laura's thing. She loved the theater. We were living overseas then, but she came stateside to visit her sister, Cherie, who lived in the city then. Laura met LaSalle and his wife, and they went to one of his early productions. That was it. I had cash to burn and could never say no to Laura."

"Small world."

"Sure is. I asked Ms. LaSalle to lunch when I first arrived. For old time's sake. She turned me down. Must remind her of the ex."

"Or she could've been busy," Lucy said. Mavis and Duncan LaSalle's divorce had been very acrimonious. *I wouldn't put it past her to give one of his friends the cold shoulder.* "Speaking of the fair Mavis, I believe she's encouraging people to find their seats."

"Okay, but parting is such sweet sorrow," he said, winking as he let her go.

CHAPTER 35

Thanks to Kendall Reese, Mavis's resident chef, the food was exquisite. Delicate salads, savory green field chowder, scallops or Netherfield filet mignon for the main course, and beautiful sides of seasonal vegetables. The Café's crusty breads complemented the meal, and the floral arrangements were breathtaking. There were many toasts throughout the meal, one of the most poignant by Lynn's father, Sol Manguilli.

"Sorcha and I knew the minute we saw Lynn last summer that something had changed. Our sweet, strong girl was happy, and there was a light in her eyes. Lynn's beauty comes from her dazzling, remarkable mother. Her strength and humanity I also attribute to Sorcha. Maybe she got a few brains from both of us, who knows." He shrugged.

"Barry and I have had the privilege of living with three extraordinary women. Now Gus has his chance. Son, I hope you know how lucky you are. Thank you for making our daughter so very happy. Our family welcomes you and wishes you many happy years together with your three precious children. Cherish every minute."

By the time her father sat down, tears were streaming down Lynn's face. Barb's too. Their brother held his wife Molly's hand. She was also crying. The only stalwart one was Sorcha, who sat ramrod straight in her chair, a soft smile on her face. Lucy watched her, remembering Barb's description of how much pain their mother was in. None of the drugs completely obliterated it, and she had insisted on minimal doses today so she could be alert and enjoy the wedding. Soon after dessert, her son Barry scooped her up, her weak, sticklike arms clinging to his neck as he carried her out.

"What a dreadful disease," Helen said, noticing Lucy's gaze.

"Yes," she said, squeezing her mother's hand.

Gus's father and sister Laurie also gave loving toasts and Tom Jacobi, his best man and former boss, rounded things off with a warm, humorous tribute to his former colleague. "I know I speak for everyone at Valley Stables when I say you're missed and will always be missed. You sure contributed in starting things off right out there. Been fun to see your new farm and think about future collaborations. You've got quite a herd over there. Good luck with Tornado, buddy. Thanks, too, for my new digs. This old bachelor is loving that beautiful house you guys left me. Harley says to tell you good luck, Spark, Ben Senior and the whole crew in Saguaro too.

"Now...Lynn, Dulcie, and Cal—are you sure you know what you're getting into? I mean, a guy from Wyoming that spends his days whispering sweet nothings in horses' ears? That's enough to scare anyone right off the ranch. I guess if you can overlook that, you'll be just fine. More than fine. You've got a great guy there, and, as Sol says, he's a very lucky man."

As Kyle led Harriet onto the dance floor, Richard found her standing alone. "May I have this dance?"

Lucy turned and smiled at him. "One of my favorites," she said, taking his hand as the band began playing Van Morrison's "Into the Mystic."

Gail nudged her sister as she spied their dad and Lucy. "Will you look at that."

"Told you they'd get it together," Weezie said. "Now I'm gonna find someone to whirl *me* around out there."

As her sister made her way across the room, a voice beside Gail said, "Don't s'pose you'd like to dance?"

Startled she turned to see Tim Miller, hand outstretched, his dark brown eyes warm. "Yes, I'd love to," she said, taking his hand.

As Tim led Gail onto the floor, Lucy spied them. "Oh, Richard, look."

"Guess there's hope that someone may pierce that prickly armor after all. Who is that handsome Laurence Olivier lookalike?"

Lucy laughed. "Oh, Richard, you are dating yourself. Laurence Olivier, really?"

"Classics never go out of date," he said, smiling down at her. "Now, you gonna fill me in? Who is he?"

"Maybe later," she said, resting her head against his chest.

"That's my girl," he said, pulling her closer.

She could feel him grow hard against her belly, and she smiled, closing her eyes. *There's no place else I'd rather be now and forever*, she thought as she gave herself to the music.

After several dances, Richard decided he should ask Helen to dance. "Good luck with that," Lucy said. "Mom's not much of a dancer."

"Well, I'll have to change that," he said, heading for her mother.

Sure enough, the Morgan charm did the trick, and Lucy watched as he led Helen onto the dance floor to the strains of "My Girl." Lucy danced with her son and then Amy and some of her friends. Lolly joined them on Sister Sledge's "We Are Family."

As the evening wore down, Amy and Rob made plans to go off with friends. Finally, as Helen, Harriet, and Kyle gathered their things to depart, Lucy decided she was ready. She said goodbye to Lynn and Gus, then checked in with Barb and Laurie to see if they or their families needed anything, then headed for the door. Richard was surrounded by family, but she caught his eyes for a second and smiled. She hugged her mother and sister, then headed for her car at the far end of the lot.

"Hey, Lucy, wait!" Richard called, coming out a side door.

She threw her things in the car, then waited until he reached her. "You sure know your way around. Where does that door lead?"

"Kitchen," he said, grinning. "I've already signed Kendall up to help Callie for Morgan's Fire's official opening next month."

"Oh, I didn't know there'd be one."

"Oh yes, very important when launching a new brand."

"You are a businessman, aren't you?"

He gazed down, giving her a quizzical look. "Hell, yeah. Didn't make all that money lounging about."

She smiled, draping her arms around his neck. "You wanted to see me?"

"Yes, mostly to ask *when* I can see you."

"Tomorrow's pretty free, and I've got work this week, but I can always find time. What were you thinking?"

"How about I take you to dinner? Teddy's been raving about all the great restaurants in Providence. Let's try a fancy one, maybe the Parkside or Al Forno?"

"You choose. I love both of those."

"Okay, then. Kendall tells me the Parkside has an innovative young chef. Good friend of hers. I'll bet she can get us a great table."

Lucy laughed. "Sounds lovely. You chat with your best buddy Kendall and let me know the time."

"Uh-oh, not jealous of Kendall, are you?"

"No."

"Good. It's just when I find a fellow foodie, there's no stopping me."

"Apparently not. Good night." She stood on tiptoes and kissed him lightly, lips closed, a friendly kiss, even though her body screamed *more!*

"Night, sweet girl. I'll call or text in the morning." With a kiss on her forehead, he opened her car door.

"You are a charmer, Richard Morgan."

He winked. "It's in the genes."

CHAPTER 36

When Lucy opened the door in her little black dress, Richard's eyes nearly popped out of his head. "Wow!"

Her neck was bare, and the dress's lacy bodice and capped sleeves needed no adornment. Margaret had chosen black stiletto heels, which were surprisingly comfortable, and teardrop earrings that caught the light every time Lucy turned her head. Her coat was draped over her arm.

"You're looking pretty wow yourself," she said, handing him her coat.

"Brunello Cucinelli," he said, hand on his chest stroking the brown jacket's rough linen.

"Am I supposed to know who that is?"

He laughed. "No, absolutely not! Rich and I went on a shopping trip in the city last year, and I ended up with this and a couple of others. He looks better in his."

"I sincerely doubt that," she said as she slipped into her coat, brushing against him.

"You know I'm not going to be able eat a thing with you in that dress, don't you?"

She laughed. "Somehow, I think you'll manage."

They chatted about the wedding and their days on the thirty-minute drive to Providence. Kendall's call to Robbie, the Parkside chef, secured them an intimate table in the quieter, interior dining area. They sat in a small booth, the alcove upholstered in muted chintz, the round table clearly designed for two.

"This is nice," Lucy said, slipping into the comfortable alcove.

"And the long tablecloth is made for playing footsie," he whispered, nodding as the waiter, who introduced himself as Frank, handed him the menu. "Could we have a wine list too?"

When the waiter departed, he asked about wine or a drink, and she waved. "Anything's fine. You choose."

"Know what you're having?"

"Some kind of seafood or maybe chicken. Oh yes, I think I'll have the coq au vin. I haven't had it in ages, and I love it."

"Good choice. Kendall recommended we order from the rotisserie menu."

"What else did your bosom buddy recommend?"

He grinned. "That's it as far as I recall. I think I'll have the pork mignon."

"Sounds delicious."

"Shall we share a salad?"

"Lovely."

"Your choice."

"I'm going to go with the Parkside. Just simple greens."

Frank returned, and Richard ordered a bottle of sauvignon blanc. After he returned and decanted and served the wine, he took their orders. Ten minutes later, he reappeared with a platter of assorted appetizers.

"Compliments of the chef. He's good friends with Ms. Reese."

"Well, well, well... Your Kendall does get around."

"And don't these look incredible?"

As they enjoyed the wonderful food, wine flowed, and they chatted amiably. "Oh, how I've missed this," he said, popping a bite of pork in his mouth. "This is the most incredible pork I've ever eaten. I must get Kendall to ask for the recipe. We're thinking of raising a few pigs, did I tell you?"

She shook her head, smiling. Richard truly enjoyed life more than anyone she knew. "I've missed this too. And the coq au vin is delicious."

"How is everything, folks?" asked a short, attractive man in a chef's coat and apron. "I'm Robbie, the executive chef."

"Truly outstanding," Richard said. "If I had a food blog, I'd be on it tonight singing your praises."

Robbie laughed. "Thanks, glad you like it."

"Thank you for the appetizers," Lucy said. "That was very kind of you."

"Of course. Don't let 'em charge you for dessert either. Enjoy."

"I wonder if *he* does private functions," Richard said, watching the chef circulate.

Lucy smiled. "I doubt it. He seems kind of busy, don't you think? Besides, between Callie and Kendall, you would appear to have enough cooks to satisfy even your insatiable appetite."

"Mmm... Speaking of my insatiable appetite, there's something else I've missed." He ran his hand up her thigh, stroking and squeezing. "Not pushing anything, I'm just saying."

She reached under the tablecloth and took his hand. "I've missed that too."

"What do you think about dessert?"

"Much as I'd love to try it, I'm stuffed. Don't think I could eat another bite."

"What say we take a short walk? There's a pretty little private park up the street. We can walk as far as that, then turn around. Help walk off a little of this dinner."

Or find a dark corner and have wild, unbridled sex, she thought as she said, "Good idea."

Lucy excused herself and went to the ladies' room while he paid the check. As she gazed at her reflection in the gilded mirror, she was surprised to see her skin flushed and pink. Was it the wine or her libido that had soared through the stratosphere the minute his hand touched her leg?

~

"THIS IS LOVELY," SHE SAID AS HE LED HER THROUGH THE WROUGHT iron gate into a small residential park, its perimeter ringed with six-foot granite stone walls. "But it looks private. Are we supposed to be in here?"

"It's open, isn't it? Teddy showed it to me when I came up for lunch last month. Pretty cool, huh?" He led her to a shaded corner along the wall.

"So is this why you chose the Parkside?"

She could see him grinning in the dark. "Caught me. I admit I suggested restaurants with interesting after-dinner strolling. Al Forno has the docks."

"Very clever," she said, wrapping her arms around his neck. "Does this fall within the 'just friends' parameters?"

"I certainly hope so," he said. Hands on her ass, he drew her close. "I like your height in those heels."

"Are you going to kiss me?" she whispered, fingers caressing his neck.

In answer, he captured her lips in a deep kiss, his tongue finding hers as his hands moved from her ass to her breasts, cupping each through the thin lace. Gently, he fingered aside the delicate cloth, his lips moving down her neck to her glorious chest, licking, kissing. Lucy arched to meet him, her breath coming in short bursts.

"Oh, oh, oh," she whispered.

"Think we dare?" he asked, voice husky.

"If we don't, I'm going to die right here." She reached down, slipping her panties off. "Can I put these in your pocket?"

"Be my guest," he said, moving one hand downward and parting her legs. He groaned as he felt her moist warmth.

Lucy's hands moved downward to his fly. "Okay if I...?"

"If you don't, I will." He kissed her hard, his fingers slipping in and out of her in delicious rhythm.

As Lucy stroked him, rubbing her body against his, Richard

grabbed hold of her, thrusting her against the smooth granite garden wall.

"Oh baby," he said, slipping the skirt of her dress up, then wrapping her legs around him.

Lucy opened up, giving herself to him, her arms around his neck. Richard grabbed her ass and drove into her hard and deep.

"I've never wanted anyone like this," he whispered as she arched, swiveled, and surged to meet him. Their frenzied rutting was soundless except for the panting of their breath as they reached a blinding crescendo of sensation. As their frenzied movements slowed, he collapsed against her, legs shaking.

Suddenly, they heard the thud of footsteps and heels clicking on cobblestones. Then the jangling of keys as someone drew nearer. Their eyes met in the glow of a nearby street light. "They're outside," he whispered, withdrawing and setting her down. He smoothed her skirt in place, then bent down to retrieve his pants.

"Only for you would I let my three thousand dollar slacks fall in the dirt," he whispered, kissing her neck as he zipped up. "Wait here," he said, fishing her panties out of his pocket. "You want to wear these, or shall I take them as a souvenir?"

Lucy snatched them. "Not funny! This is crazy! Screwing in the park at our ages? Are we nuts? I'm thirty-nine and you're—"

"Don't say it, babe. I feel like a young stallion, and you look like a teenager."

"And I'm acting like one too!" she said, slipping on her coat, which she had tossed on a nearby bench.

"Are you sorry?" He pulled her close and kissed her softly. "'Cause I'm not."

"No, just surprised at myself. I've always been the put-together one of my family. Mom's a bohemian, always has been, as are Harriet and Hazel. Clara's...well, Clara's sweet but spacey."

"Well, from my perspective, you're still put together, with a touch of wild woman. Gotta let that loose sometimes."

"Only with you. Come on. Let's get back to the car before I'm tempted to let loose again."

Later, when Richard pulled into her driveway, he parked, then turned to her. "Looks like the kids are home."

"Yes, and they're not alone. You're welcome to come in and say hi."

"Ordinarily, I'd say yes, but I've got an early morning tomorrow, and I want to savor tonight."

She smiled, leaning over to kiss him softly. "Thanks for dinner. It was wonderful."

"Yes, it was, but nothing compared to after dinner. I'm not going to analyze, categorize, or try to figure out where tonight fits in our friendship. I'm just gonna be glad it happened and hope for more."

"Me too."

"Want me to walk you to the door?"

"Thanks, but you stay put. I think I'm safe."

"Night, my girl."

"Night," she said, slipping out and closing the door.

As Richard watched her walk away, he sighed. *Don't know where this is headed, but I know I can't let her go again.*

"Hey, Mom, how was your date with Mr. Morgan?" Amy called from the family room. She and two of her friends were watching a movie, bowls of popcorn in their laps.

"It was just dinner." *Who am I kidding?*

"Where'd you go?"

"Providence. We ate at the Parkside. Food was amazing. I'll have to take you there sometime. Hey, ladies."

"Hey, Ms. Brennan... I mean, Winthrop," Celia Carney called. "You're looking hot!" Delia Harper, their companion, waved.

"What happened to your dress, Mom? It's ripped on the side," Amy said.

Surprised, Lucy gazed down. Sure enough, the seam was split just below the waist, a jagged tear beside it. "Darn," she said. "I caught it on a chair, but thought it was okay." *Liar, liar, pants on fire!*

"It can probably be mended. Take it to Morelli's. They'll fix it good as new," Celia said. "My mom takes all her clothes there."

"Good idea," Lucy said.

"That was a cool party yesterday, wasn't it?'" Celia said, receiving looks from her companions, who clearly wanted to get back to the movie. Celia often worked weddings for Mavis, and she'd been serving at Gus and Lynn's reception.

Lucy nodded. "It was lovely."

"And all kinds of hookups. First, of course, there was you and Mr. Morgan. Cutest couple in the world!"

"Celia!" Amy said, giving her friend a sharp look. "They're friends."

Undaunted, Celia went on. "And you could've knocked me over with a feather when I saw Tim Miller leaving with that Morgan lady. Is she even his age?"

All of Amy's friends were in love with the much older, handsome furniture maker. Lucy decided that no comment might be the wisest choice.

"Well, I'm going to head up to bed and let you girls get back to your movie. Night."

She smiled walking up the stairs. She was happy for Gail. *Now let's hope if they get involved, he doesn't break her heart.*

CHAPTER 37

"We can't keep a wild horse cooped up like this for three days," Richard said as he, Weezie, and Dennis Farrell watched Tornado pace. Occasionally, the enormous black stallion paused and kicked against a wall or the stall door.

"I'd recommend leaving him in, sir," Dennis said. "Stall's in good shape, and the guys can clean around him."

"I disagree. He's got to go out at least for a few hours."

"It's dangerous both ways, but it'll be the devil to get him back in tonight."

"I can do it," Weezie said.

"Absolutely not," Richard said. "It's my idea. I'll lead him out."

Dennis shook his head. "Let me get a couple of apples."

Richard stood at the stall door, talking softly to the gigantic animal. Unlike most mustangs, Tornado was many hands taller and stockier than the rest of the herd. "Hey, boy, it's okay. Nice out today. Here, boy."

Dennis handed him several apples, which he pocketed, keeping one in his hand. "Here, boy, look what I've got."

Tornado loved apples and immediately came to the door. Richard offered the fruit on his outstretched flat hand. "That's it," he said, gently reaching down to take the lead as Tornado gobbled up the fruit, stray bits falling in the straw.

Richard took another apple from his pocket, one hand on the lead. "Open the door," he said softly. "And Weezie, stand back."

"That's right, come on, boy," he said, slowly backing up, keeping the apple just out of reach, the lead tight at his side. Tornado advanced, eyes never leaving the object of his desire. As they stepped through the barn door into the sunlight, Richard offered the second apple, then slowly walked toward the nearest corral.

The third apple now in his hand, they'd reached the open corral gate. "Just a little farther, boy. That's right."

"Don't go inside, sir. Just toss the apple. He'll go after it."

Ignoring Dennis, Richard took three steps into the enclosure, the apple still in his hand.

As the gate closed behind them, the apple was forgotten as Tornado realized he was trapped. He let out a scream and reared up, hooves flying.

"Jesus Christ," Dennis yelled. "Richard, get out!"

"Dad, come on! Climb the fence!" Weezie cried, but the horse blocked his escape. As Richard stepped back, he stumbled, bent over as the apple rolled out of his hand. Tornado reared up again. When he slammed down, his front right hoof grazed the side of Richard's head, knocking him to the hard-packed ground.

"Daddy!" Weezie screamed as the horse trotted to the opposite end of the corral.

Dennis swung open the gate. "Get ready to slam it shut," he said, running to his boss and lifting him onto his shoulders.

Tornado stood as far away from them as he could get, calm now, watching.

"Call 911!" Dennis cried, carrying him to a grassy spot near the barn.

CHAPTER 38

Rich met her in the hospital hallway. "Thanks for coming, Lucy. He's okay. A concussion, no broken bones. Because he was unconscious for a while they want to keep him overnight to make sure there's no brain swelling."

Tear sprang to her eyes. "Oh, Rich, I'm so sorry."

"He's gonna be fine. My sisters are with him."

Lucy's eyes met his. *How alike they are, father and son.* Rich's eyes held the same warmth and light as his father's. Richard always said that his eldest was more like his mother, but in every way except coloring, he was like his dad.

"I'll wait out here," she said.

Rich touched her hand. "Don't be silly. He was kicked in the head, he's not dead. I'm sure he wants to see you."

As she peeked in through the door, Gail rose and came out to greet her. "He's been asking for you. Sleeping now."

"I thought you kept people awake after concussions?"

Gail shrugged. "They check him every fifteen minutes and will observe him overnight. I guess that's the protocol these days."

"What happened?"

Gail shook her head. "I wasn't there, but against Dennis's strong objections, pigheaded Dad insisted on taking Tornado out. Have you seen him? Huge black stallion, wildest of the bunch."

Lucy nodded.

"Gus is the only person the horse will let near him. Dennis was planning to keep him in the barn till Gus gets back, but you know Dad. Thinks he's everything, including a horse whisperer, apparently.

"Anyway, Tornado reared up and Dad fell. Hoof came down and caught the side of his head. Tornado wasn't trying to hurt him. He was just spooked. Rich and I think we should get rid of him."

"Well, we're not," Weezie said, stepping into the hall. "It wasn't Tornado's fault."

Gail threw up her hands. "I can't talk about this now. I'm going to the cafeteria for coffee. Anyone want anything?" She started down the hall without waiting for their answer.

"I'm going to the ladies room, Weezie said. "Did you want to sit with him?"

Lucy hugged her. "Of course, you go."

He looked impossibly small and frail in the oversized hospital bed. Lucy wondered if they'd had the enormous bed brought in especially for him. A bandage was wrapped around his head. She sat in the chair beside him and took his hand. He stirred, but his eyes remained closed.

"Oh, Richard, what have you done to yourself now?" she said, leaning down, kissing his hand. "I was so frightened, but here you are. You're going to be fine. You have to be fine. Please, my love."

Lucy rested her head on the bed, continuing to hold his hand. Doctors, family, and nurses came and went all day, but Lucy rarely left his side. Occasionally, Richard woke and gave her a sleepy smile before nodding off again. People brought her food, but she barely ate. When a nurse or one of his children was there, she would pop out to the ladies' room or to make a call to her kids. When she told Amy and Rob that she was spending the night in the hospital, both decided to stay at their dad's.

Just before dinner, Dr. Freeland, the neurologist, came in. The others had gone home, and Lucy sat alone with Richard. The petite blonde thirty-something physician spent several minutes reading the chart, then spoke to him. "Richard? Richard, can you hear me?"

He opened his eyes, gave her a glazed look, then closed them again. Freeland turned to the nurse. "He should be more wakeful. Continue to check him every fifteen minutes throughout the night. If you can't wake him, have them call me."

"Is something wrong?" Lucy asked.

"You're not family, are you, Ms. Winthrop?"

"No."

Freeland's eyes were warm as she gazed down at her. "I'm sorry. I really can't discuss it with you."

"But his son said he was going to be fine."

"As I say, patient confidentiality prevents me from discussing his condition with anyone but immediate family."

"That would be me," a voice said behind them, and Ben Morgan stepped into the room. "I'm his son, Dr. Morgan."

Freeland turned, her eyes registering both surprise and interest. "Oh? Do you practice around here, Dr. Morgan?"

"Philadelphia."

Lucy watched the two, guessing them to be about the same age. She couldn't remember if Ben had a girlfriend, but like all the Morgan men, he was gorgeous and probably had women falling all over him. She let go of Richard's hand and stood up. "Ben, I'm so glad you're here."

He turned to Dr. Freeland. "So what's going on?"

"He sustained a concussion. He was hit in the left temple and was unconscious for a number of minutes. We've been watching him closely. I would expect by this time that he'd be a bit more wakeful. If nothing changes, we'll do more tests in the morning."

"Why not now? Has he had a CT scan?"

"Yes, and it was normal. If things don't improve, we'll do an MRI in the morning, but with rest, I fully expect him to rebound. As you know, the brain needs time to settle after a trauma."

They talked for a few more minutes, then Lucy resumed her place by Richard's side. After Freeland left, Ben came to the other side of the bed.

"Hey, Dad," he said, hand resting on his father's cheek.

Richard opened his eyes. "Hey, son. Am I dreaming?"

Ben smiled. "Nope, it's me in the flesh."

"Were you coming today and I forgot?"

"Gail called after your run-in with the horse."

"Aw, shoot. It was nothing. And here's Lucy too." He turned loving eyes on her.

"You're looking better," she said. *Only a tiny lie.* He actually looked ashen.

"You look as beautiful as ever, my girl."

Lucy blushed.

Ben gazed down, giving him a critical look. "At least your vision's okay. How's your head feel?"

"Fine. I feel fine, just tired. Hospitals make me tired. Why am I still here, anyway?"

"Observation. Have you had anything to eat?"

Richard gave her a quizzical look.

Lucy said, "A little water and a cracker. He's been sleeping most of the time."

"Excuse me. I'm going to try to catch the doc."

Ben disappeared, and Lucy sat down, taking his hand.

"Isn't it time for you to go home?"

"Maybe later. For now, I'm staying with you."

"Good," he said, closing his eyes.

Ten minutes later, Ben appeared, followed by a nurse with an IV stand. "Someone will be back shortly to set this up," she said, setting the stand next to the bed.

"I'll be damned if he goes all night with no fluid or nourishment," Ben said. "I'll hook it up myself if they aren't back soon."

Ben's next foray was to the nurse's station to request recliners. Miraculously, two appeared just before midnight. "Doctor has given permission for you both to stay," the nurse said. "But we need to get in next to the bed to check him."

"No problem," Ben said. "Lucy, you take the other side of the bed, and I'll go over here by the window."

"Thank you," she said, settling down, taking Richard's hand in hers, then pulling a thin hospital blanket over her.

She drifted off, sometimes waking when they examined Richard, sometimes sleeping through it, dimly aware of Ben's questions and oversight, reassured by his presence. When she woke in the morning, Richard was asleep and Ben was sitting, reading his chart.

"How is he?"

"Still sleeping. I'm going to insist on the MRI this morning."

"What is it?"

"I'm not sure. Neurology is way out of my area, but I know this much sleeping isn't good. I'm going to make some calls. My sisters and brother should be in soon. Ava's dropping the kids at a sitter's, and Teddy said he's coming later. I'm wondering if we should get Pam down here too."

"Oh, Ben, is it that serious?"

"I don't know. Listen, hang tight. Do you need a break?"

"No, I'm staying with him."

"Good. I'd rather he's not alone. Someone can spell you later. I'll be back soon, I promise." He hurried out, closing the door.

CHAPTER 39

The room was impossibly quiet after Ben's departure, Richard's gentle breathing the only sound she heard. *Eerie for a hospital where it was never quiet.* Lucy's heart ached. She had seen the worry in Ben's eyes. *He's scared. What is he not telling me?*

Exhausted and heartsick, she took Richard's hand in both of hers. "Come on, darling. Come back to me, please. How can we get married if you don't wake up? Yes, yes, yes, I want to marry you, tomorrow if you want. I've been a silly fool to make you wait so long. I love you so much. If you wake up, I can tell you, show you, whatever you want. Please, my darling. I can't live without you. Please, please, please."

Suddenly, she felt a gentle pressure on her hand and looked up to find his eyes open. "Hey, baby, I've just had the most wonderful dream."

"I'm so glad to see you," she said, squeezing his hand.

He gave her a crooked, sleepy smile. "In my dream, you said yes. Made me the happiest man in the world."

Lucy sat up straight. "It wasn't a dream."

"Oh?" His eyes seemed clearer now as he woke.

"I did say yes. Yes, yes, yes, I'll marry you."

He grinned, reaching out to touch her cheek with his gentle fingers. "Have you been here all night, baby?"

She nodded.

"Poor girl. Was I pestering you? Did I propose again?"

"No, but I'm hoping you will."

"Just let me out of this damn bed, and I'll get down on my knee right now!"

"Absolutely not!"

He grabbed hold of the IV pole. "Why the hell am I hooked up to this contraption?"

"To keep you hydrated."

He sat up and swung his legs over the side of the bed, then faltered, clearly dizzy.

"Okay, too fast," she said. "You rest until Ben and the doctor get here."

"Nonsense," he grumbled, lying back down. "At least let's crank up this thing so I'm sitting."

She reached down and found the button to raise the bed.

Once sitting up, he patted the mattress beside him. "That's better. Want to sit up here?"

"I'm not sure that's allowed."

"It is if I say so. They took all the trouble to order this super-duper big bed. Least we can do is fill it."

"How did that happen?" she asked, carefully sliding in beside him.

"Standing order. Whenever a Morgan is hospitalized, they get 'the bed.'"

"Really?"

He chuckled. "No, but Gail and Rich would have requested it. We did the same thing for Laura and when I broke my leg ten years ago. We all like big beds and comfort."

Lucy took his hand and rested her head on his shoulder. "You are something else, Richard Morgan."

"I'm glad you're here. Sorry about the outfit," he said, straightening his johnny. "We've gotta find my clothes."

"Not till the doctor sees you and says you can go. Ben wants you to have more tests."

"Well, that's not happening."

"Dad, what are you doing?" Gail said as she and Weezie came in, followed by Ava, Wolfie, and Rich.

Lucy attempted to hop off the bed, but Richard held her hand, preventing it.

"Sitting with my girl and waiting to get the hell out of here."

Rich gazed at Lucy. "Where's Ben?"

"He said he had to make some calls."

Richard gazed from one of his children to the other. "Why are all of you here anyway?"

"Because we're worried about you Daddy," Ava said. "Now shouldn't you be lying down?"

"No!" he said, gripping Lucy's hand tighter.

"Pam just called. She's on her way," Ava said to no one in particular.

"Teddy too," Weezie said.

Their father scowled. "I'm sitting right here, you know. I'm not deaf."

"Everyone wants to see you," Gail said, smiling at him.

Richard shook his head. "This is just plain nuts. You all know that I'm never happier than when I have you all together, but I sure as hell am not entertaining you in this godawful place in my polka-dot dress." He pulled a blanket over his knees.

"No one needs entertaining, Daddy," Weezie said.

"And no one needs fussing over. I got a kick in the head, but I'm fine. I'm ready to blow this pop stand, and I need my clothes."

Ben stepped in, a grin on his face. "Not until Dr. Freeland examines you."

Richard looked over at Lucy. "Another one? This is why people don't have large families anymore."

Ben studied him. "You're looking better, Dad. Fluids must've done you some good."

"Course I look better. I've got my girlfriend beside me and most of my favorite people around me. Now where is this Dr. Freeland? I want to go home."

Lucy smiled. Ben was right. The color had returned to Richard's cheeks, and he was alert and full of his usual energy. Much as she did not want to leave his side, it appeared that the worst was over. He was surrounded by family, and she desperately needed a shower. She squeezed Richard's hand, and before he could stop here, she slid off the bed.

"I'm going to head home for a shower and change of clothes. I'll check in later, I promise."

"First sensible word I've heard all day. I'm right behind you," Richard said. As she bent to kiss his forehead, he whispered, "Sorry we got interrupted. More later."

"Looking forward to it," she said, then turning to say goodbye to the others.

"Thanks, Lucy," Ben said. "We'll get him home and let you know what the doc says."

She hugged each one, then slipped out just as Teddy and Pam Morgan came down the hallway. *What a loving family*, she mused, greeting them too, then departing.

CHAPTER 40

That afternoon, Lucy stopped by the farm to visit with Richard and his family. They invited her to dinner, but she declined, saying she'd check in the next morning. She'd barely seen Amy and Rob for two days, and she had a million things to do.

Surrounded by family, Richard seemed overwhelmed, distracted, and tired. While he wanted her to stay, he understood. "I'll get you to myself soon," he said, kissing her as they said goodbye in the farmhouse mudroom. "Ridiculous that this is the only place we can be alone."

Her fingers stroked his cheeks. "Rest up and enjoy your wonderful family."

"They're all leaving day after tomorrow. Can we have a date?"

She laughed. "Yes, of course. Let me know."

"I'll think of somewhere really special."

"Bye," she said, giving him one last hug.

Lucy gazed up at her. "I hope so! Between the wedding guests and the Morgan clan, the village population exploded."

Lolly nodded. "It was a fun wedding. Although, no eligible bachelors. I despair of ever finding someone."

"Don't give up! He's out there somewhere. Now, these bills aren't going to pay themselves. I have Wolfie's check, but I doubt we'll see him today. I'll take it home and slip it under the apartment door."

"What's he up to?"

"Hanging out with his brothers and hovering over his dad, I'd imagine."

"Wolfie doesn't strike me as the hovering type," Lolly said.

Lucy smiled. "You're probably right."

"How *are* things with his dad, anyway?"

"Didn't I just say I have bills to pay?"

"Just answer me that one question and I'll leave you alone. Promise."

"They're good." Lucy swallowed, then decided, *what the heck. It might be good to tell someone.* "I said yes."

"To? Oh my God, you didn't?" Lolly jumped up, clapping her hands. She grabbed a nearby chair and came around to sit beside her. "Spill, and I want to hear every detail."

Bill forgotten, she said, "There aren't a lot of details. I said yes when he was sleeping. He woke up, thought it was a dream, and I said it again. Then his family piled in, and we haven't had a moment alone since."

"What? Well, when are you going to see him?"

"Tomorrow night. We'll see how that goes."

"Where? What are you doing?"

"Not sure."

"Geez, this is killing me!"

"You? What about me?"

"Sure...of course... Well... What do you think?"

"That if he asks again or still wants to marry me, I'm in."

"What changed your mind?"

"I've been leaning that way for weeks, and I've missed him like crazy, but then when I thought I might lose him the other night... That did it."

"Well, congratulations!"

"Not yet. And mum's the word. Please don't tell a soul."

Lolly hugged her. "No worries there, partner."

LUCY MET LYNN FOR LUNCH AT THE CAFÉ FRIDAY, THE BABY IN A carrier beside them. "Family gone?"

"Yes," Lynn said, her voice wistful. "I miss them. The Caseys were super helpful, Barb too. It took a lot out of Mom, but she was really happy to be here."

"Little Sorcha's an angel," Lucy said, gazing down at the sleeping infant.

"She really is, except at two in the morning. Then her fine set of lungs gets a workout. Poor Gus. I can take a nap during the day, but he's going back to work Monday. I hate to have him around those unpredictable horses when he's half-asleep."

"It gets better," Lucy said.

"Thanks for having lunch with me. I was so sorry to say goodbye to Polly and her family. I was even sad to say goodbye to Phyllis, her mom, who can drive you crazy."

"They don't live too far from here, do they?"

Lynn smiled. "Forty-five minutes. Phyllis is already planning weekly trips to check in."

"Oh, boy. They're all loving people, though, aren't they?"

Lynn sighed. "Yes, we are very fortunate. I wonder if I'll find good friends here."

Lucy reached over and patted her hand. "I guarantee it! I know we're old ladies, but you can count on me and Harriet. And you'll meet moms at the kids' school. Just takes time."

"I hope so. Sorry... This may be a bit of postpartum depression speaking."

"Perfectly normal."

"I've always felt connected wherever I lived, you know? To friends, to a job. Of course, I have Gus and the kids and know I'm so, so lucky. It's just I feel like I've been swallowed up and there's nothing left of me or for me."

"Also perfectly normal. That too will change. And if you're wanting a job, Merlin's Closet can always use a hand."

"Dulcie and Cal's school asked me about part-time work, but I don't think I'm ready."

"Don't push. That's my advice. With the baby, your mom, and two kids, you've got a lot on your plate.

"And, Lynn, when you're ready, you'll find 'me time.' There are so many options. Sara, Rich Morgan's sometime-girlfriend, runs a yoga studio in town. Her classes are great. And there's always something going on at our library—book clubs, cooking classes, you name it." Lucy reached over and patted Lynn's hand as Milly, the waitress, appeared, pad and pencil in hand. "Hey, gals, what can I get you?"

As she drove home, Lucy's cell phone rang. "Hey, baby," Richard said. "Are we still on for tonight?"

"Of course. What's the dress code?"

"Casual. Wear one of your sexy pairs of jeans. Come to think of it, anything you wear is sexy. Wear whatever you like. Pick you up at seven?"

"I'm looking forward to it. Are you sure you're up to driving?"

"I'm gonna pretend I didn't hear that. See you soon."

CHAPTER 41

"Where are we going?" Lucy asked for the fifth time since they left Somers and headed south toward Horseshoe Crab Cove.

"It's a secret," Richard said.

"I know, but can't I have a hint?"

"You'll see soon enough."

Lucy was surprised when they drove straight through the village without stopping. Out of town now, he took the east road that wound around, eventually ending at Millers' Farm at the peninsula's southeast point. Puzzled, she looked over her shoulder, wondering if he had a picnic basket in the backseat. Nothing. She'd just settled back in her seat when he turned off at the entrance to Cove Spa and Resort. "What are you up to, Richard Morgan?"

"Patience, my girl," he said.

As Netherfield loomed straight ahead of them, he turned south and followed a narrow lane until it reached a clearing where the smallest of the property's cottages was nestled among the trees. Lucy hadn't been to Laurel Cottage since her teenage years, when Lolly would throw parties there.

"The Caseys stayed here for the wedding," she said.

"Well, it's ours tonight, baby. Come on."

Mouth agape, she took his hand as he led her up onto the porch. The windows cast a soft glow in the growing twilight.

Richard opened the front door. "Welcome, my love."

Like all Mavis's properties, the cottage was exquisitely decorated in muted colors, with comfortable upholstered furnishings, tasteful artwork on the walls, wrought iron lamps, and antique chairs and tables. Candles flickered on every surface, the only lighting except for a thin ray of soft light from the kitchen. He pointed to a table for two set with delicate linens and fine china. "Our friend Kendall has left us a wonderful meal."

"Richard, how did you?"

"But first, come here, my sweet girl." He led her to the hearth, where a warm fire burned brightly. He indicated a small chair covered with chintz in a soft blue-green cabbage rose pattern. "Sit, please, if you would."

Lucy smiled, complying as he grabbed a small pillow from another chair and flopped it on the floor.

"Concession to an *old* man," he said, kneeling. Out of his pocket came the familiar velvet box. He held it in one hand, taking hers in the other.

Lucy gazed down at his beautiful eyes so full of emotion. "Can I say yes now?"

"No! Not until I say the words again. Lucy, my beloved girl. Will you marry me?"

"Yes!" She leaped into his arms, knocking him back onto the soft kilim rug. "Yes, yes, yes!"

Richard blinked, and for an instant, she thought she might have hurt him. "Oh, sweetheart, are you okay?" She cupped his face.

He rolled them over so they lay side by side, then pushed up on one elbow. "Can I put this on your finger before you get away?" He popped open the box, revealing the exquisite ring. She gave him her hand, and he slipped it on. "There, now I feel okay."

"I love you so much," she said, kissing him. "How did you arrange all this?"

He grinned. "You forget, Mavis and I go way back. It's ours for the night."

"But my kids, I can't."

"Lolly fixed it. They're staying with friends."

"They know about this?"

"Not exactly. Just that you'd be out late and you'd feel better if they were taken care of."

What must they be thinking? she mused, but suddenly, it seemed okay. Her kids would be okay and would be thrilled to see her happy. The pipedream to see her reconciled with Rob had died, and they liked Richard and his family. *Yes, everything will be okay.*

"You are amazing, and I love you very much, Richard Morgan," she whispered, kissing him deeply. As their lips parted, she began trailing kisses down his neck.

"You hungry?" he asked, voice husky with desire.

"I'm sure Kendall's prepared something delicious, but not as delicious as this."

"Mmm... I like the sound of that, fiancée of mine. Shall we find the bedroom?"

"I don't know. This rug feels pretty comfy." She smiled, her eyes soft. "We have all night and the rest of our lives to find the bedroom."

He pulled her closer. "The rug it is."

PLEASE READ ON FOR SAMPLE CHAPTERS OF *TIM'S HANDS*, BOOK TWO IN the *Morgan's Fire* series!

TIM'S HANDS

I am so excited to bring you a sneak preview of Tim's Hands, *book two in the Morgan's Fire series which debuts in July of 2019. Gail and Tim's story is filled with angst, heartache, and, of course, the healing power of love and family. The new and familiar characters of Morgan's Fire continue to live and work in the beautiful New England seaside community of Horseshoe Crab Cove. Obstacles abound for these lovers, from the sudden appearance of Tim's long-lost fiancée to Gail's fear of another broken heart. Please read on and let me know what you think!*

Chapter 1

"This is beautiful work," Gail Morgan said, running her hand over the surface of the cherry coffee table.

"Thanks," Tim Miller said. "Cherry's a great wood to work with."

Gail held her breath as he ran large, rough hands over the smooth tabletop inches from her own. She was there in the workshop to buy a wedding present, but the object of her desire was the man, not the table. Finally, she said, "I don't know Gus and Lynn well, but I'm sure they'll love this. My dad was thinking of buying a matching piece. Have you anything that might work?"

His dark eyes watched her. "Sure, I can find something, or make it. End tables? Maybe a small buffet, or a side table with drawers?"

"Those all sound great. I'll check with him. He might like to come by, or I could bring him?"

After one dance at Gus and Lynn Casey's recent wedding, Gail had been head over heels, which wasn't at all like her. *I am the steady, sensible Morgan, not some crazed teeny bopper!* She knew the woodworker's reputation. *Every woman in the village—hell, every teenager in the village—is in love with the man some called the Heathcliff of Horseshoe Crab Cove. Ridiculous of me to entertain one speck of hope!* Still, unable to keep away, she had visited his workshop, Tim's Hands, twice in the past two weeks.

"He's getting married too, I hear."

"Who?" Startled, she realized she'd lost the thread of their conversation.

"Your dad."

"Oh yes, that," she said, relieved to find a topic about which she could say something coherent. "My siblings and I are thrilled. It's been twenty years since we lost our mom. We all love Lucy."

"Ms. Brennan's good people. Or does she go by Winthrop now?"

"Yes, she does."

"Her mom's one of the Darn Yarners. Good friend of my mom's."

She nodded. "Yes, the Yarners. Quite a group."

"That's the village for you. It's one huge family, in case you hadn't noticed. Great most of the time, unless you're a private person."

"Which you are?"

Surprised, he gave her a sharp look, a glint of fire in the dark eyes.

Gail blanched. "Oh, I'm sorry... I didn't mean to imply. I mean... I don't know you."

He grinned. "No worries. Yes, I'm a private person. Probably why I've chosen jobs where I spend most of my time alone."

"Well, to that end, I'll let you get back to work. I'll chat with my dad and get back to you about the other piece or pieces, but I'm definitely taking the table."

"Now?"

"If it's ready."

"Or I can deliver it to them?"

Gail thought for a minute, afraid to meet those gorgeous eyes again. "Why don't I pay you and leave it here for a day or two? I'd like to get a card to attach to it. Then I'd be grateful if you could deliver it so I don't scratch it. I'll bring the address and the card by."

He smiled, watching her fumble with her purse and finally extract her checkbook.

She met his eyes and nearly swooned. "You do take checks, don't you?" *Get a grip, Gail Morgan! You're not some silly schoolgirl, and besides, he's miles older than you.*

"Not gonna bounce, is it?"

"No!"

He grinned, throwing up his hands. "Kidding."

"Do I make it out to you or Tim's Hands?"

"Either's fine. All goes into the same bank account."

Her accountant voice almost said, *better watch how you handle your business profits*, but she kept silent, hastily scribbling out the check and handing it to him. "You know you could get double what you're asking for that."

"Maybe."

"I'll be in touch."

"Great."

As she hurried out of the workshop, Gail passed Coop Merrick, the blacksmith who shared the barn with Tim. He called, "Hey," but she barely heard him, so anxious was she to get out to the street where she could breathe. When she stepped outside, she leaned against the rough barn wall catching her breath, remembering that she needed to speak to Coop about the lamps he was making for her father and Lucy. *Next time*, she thought, *unless I faint dead away the minute I lay eyes on Tim Miller!*

Middle daughter of Richard Morgan, Gail lived with her dad and sister Weezie on the farm and vineyard, Morgan's Fire. Her father's estate lay just outside the village of Horseshoe Crab Cove, or the Cove, as the locals called it. Gail worked for her dad doing publicity for many of his businesses, most recently the vineyard they were endeavoring to bring back to life on the north end of the vast property.

Twenty-six years old, Gail had dated only sporadically. One college relationship had been serious, but ended with a broken heart. Hers. She vowed never again, but that was before she'd laid eyes on Tim Miller. One glance at the tall, ruggedly handsome woodworker and lobsterman and she was gone.

They'd met at the Lab where her sister Ava and husband Dan worked. Tim did occasional jobs for his aunt, Grace Childs Straley, the director. Just in from a run up the river, he was dressed in yellow bib overalls and a red-and-black-plaid flannel shirt, his face red from the wind and sun, hair drenched, two buckets filled with seawater and crabs in his hands. As Gail rounded the main building, they ran smack dab into each other. Water and sea creatures sloshed down her front as she screamed, "Oh, oh, oh!"

Her sister Ava flew out of the office. "Wow!" was all she said.

"Wow? How about yuck!" Gail said. "I have a whole day of meetings, and now I smell like dead fish!"

Then she looked up at the man in front of her, and that was it. *Crash, boom!* Lightning struck.

Since then, she'd seen him briefly at a New Year's Eve party she'd attended with her sister Weezie, but aside from a nod and hello, they hadn't connected. Then he approached her at Gus and Lynn's wedding and extended his hand. "Can I have this dance? Not carrying a bucket of water tonight, no fish in my pocket, promise. Never did get to apologize that day 'cause you ran off so quick."

Gail had blushed, taking his hand. "I guess I might have overreacted just a tad."

Then, like a fairy tale, he had swept her into his strong arms. "You wouldn't be the first."

She'd decided not to wonder what he'd meant by that and to enjoy the moment. And enjoy she had. Since then, she'd played Van

Morrison's iconic "Into the Mystic" countless times, reliving every second of their dance.

"Cute redhead," Coop called to Tim as his shop mate carried a pile of wood in from the back.

"Is it red?"

Coop grinned. "I'd say so. Or auburn?" He watched Tim, whom he'd known since grade school. Girls fell all over him, but his friend seldom reciprocated. "You interested?"

"She's buying a table."

"That doesn't mean you can't be interested."

"She's just a kid."

Coop grinned. "Doesn't look like a kid to me."

"Who knows. Certainly not me."

Tim tossed the wood in a growing pile. *Deer in the headlights, more like it, and a beautiful one at that.* There *was* something about Gail Morgan. Ever since he'd dumped water all over her designer suit, he hadn't been able to put her out of his mind. *Maybe it's 'cause she's new in town and not one of the silly gaggle of girls that sometimes follow me.* It was embarrassing.

He didn't know much about the Morgans except what he heard around town or at the dinner table. His sister Karen's best friend was Kyle Morgan's fiancée, Harriet, and Tim liked the couple. Since he'd set up his practice, the young vet had made several calls to treat horses at their parents' stables, and he and Harriet had been to dinner at the farm. *Good people.*

"So you could still ask her out. What's five or six years matter?" Coop called.

"Try ten or fifteen."

"No."

"Doesn't matter. Not interested." *Liar, liar, pants on fire!* He was interested, for the first time since Isabel had disappeared.

"She's not coming back, buddy," Coop said for the hundredth

time over the last few years.

"Izzy has nothing to do with it. Now can we drop this, please? I've got a shitload of work to do."

As he began a rough sand of an oak end table, he wondered, as he did every day, *Where the hell is Izzy? Why did she leave? Why hasn't she been in touch?* And, at his darkest hours, *Is she alive?*

Get *Tim's Hands*!

ALSO BY M. LEE PRESCOTT

Contemporary Romance

Morgan's Run Romances

Book 1: *Emma's Dream*

Book 2: *Lang's Return*

Book 3: *Jeb's Promise*

Book 4: *Rose's Choice*

Book 5: *Hope's Wonder*

Book 6: *Ruthie's Love*

Book 7: *Polly's Heart*

Book 8: *Kyle's Journey*

Book 9: *Gus' Home*

Book 10: *A Valley Christmas*

Morgan's Fire Romances

Book 1: *Lucy's Hearth*

Book 2: *Tim's Hands*

Book 3: *Pam's Garden*

Book 4: *Rich's Dilemma*

Well-Loved Romances

Widow's Island

Hestor's Way

Mystery

The Ricky Steele Mysteries

Book 1: *Prepped to Kill*

Book 2: *Gadfly*

Book 3: *Lost in Spindle City*

Book 4: *Poof!*

Also, featuring Ricky Steele:

Jigsaw

Roger and Bess Mysteries

Book 1: *A Friend of Silence*

Book 2: *In the Name of Silence*

Book 3: *The Silence of Memory*

Book 4: *Silencing the Pen* (coming in 2020!)

Young Adult Historical Romance

Song of the Spirit

A NOTE FROM THE AUTHOR

I am so happy to bring you Lucy and Richard's love story! This marks the first of the *Morgan's Fire* books and also previews number two, *Tim's Hands*—coming in summer of 2019. A contemporary romance series, the *Morgan's Fire* follows Helen, Harriet and a host of strong, resilient women—and men—across the country to the New England coastal town of Horseshoe Crab Cove. Thank you so much for reading *Lucy's Hearth* and exploring Horseshoe Crab Cove with me. What fun it is to set this book and this series on my home turf, the craggy New England coast, in a beautiful, *fictional* village filled with colorful, vibrant characters.

If you like *Lucy's Hearth* and are willing to write an Amazon review, I would be very grateful. If you would like to sign up for future book releases, giveaways and occasional notices about my books, please visit my Author Website and sign up for my newsletter and follow me on BookBub. I promise I will not share your address, nor will I flood you with emails. Do visit my site to read more about my books and hear what's next.

Finally, this book has been revised, proofed, and edited many, many times, but my intrepid assistants and I are human, so if you spot a typo, please email me at mleeprescott@gmail.com, and I will fix it.

Warm wishes,
M. Lee

ABOUT THE AUTHOR

M. Lee Prescott is the author of dozens of works of fiction for adults, young adults, and children, among them *Prepped to Kill, Gadfly, Lost in Spindle City,* and *Poof!* (Ricky Steele Mysteries), *A Friend of Silence, In the Name of Silence,* and *The Silence of Memory* (Roger and Bess Mysteries), *Jigsaw,* and *Song of the Spirit,* and her contemporary romance series, *Morgan's Run.* And now there is *Morgan's Fire* and book two, *Tim's Hands!* Lee is thrilled to be launching three Morgan's Fire titles in 2019. In addition to her fiction, her nonfiction books are published by Heinemann, and she has written numerous articles in the field of literacy education. Lee is a professor of education at a small New England liberal arts college, where she teaches reading and writing pedagogy. Her current research focuses on mindfulness and connections to reading and writing. She regularly teaches abroad, most recently in Singapore.

Lee has lived in southern California (loved those Laguna nights!), Chapel Hill, North Carolina, and various spots in Massachusetts and Rhode Island. Currently, she resides in Massachusetts on a beautiful river, where she canoes, swims, and watches an incredible variety of wildlife pass by. She is the mother of two grown sons and spends lots of time with them, their beautiful wives, and her beloved grandchildren. When not teaching or writing, Lee's passions revolve around family, yoga (Kripalu is a second home), swimming, sharing mindfulness with children and adults, and walking.

Lee loves to hear from readers. Email her at mleeprescott@ gmail.com, and visit her website to hear the latest and sign up for her newsletters!

AUTHOR WEBPAGE AND NEWSLETTER SIGN-UP
FOLLOW ME ON BOOKBUB!